BOOKS BY I

BEECHWOOD HARBOR MAGIC MYSTERIES

Murder's a Witch

Twice the Witch

Witch Slapped

Witch Way Home

Along Came a Ghost

Lucky Witch (Fall 2017)

BEECHWOOR HARBOR GHOST MYSTERIES

The Ghost Hunter Next Door

Ghosts Gone Wild

INTRODUCTION

Holly's faced some serious challenges following her banishment from the supernatural community but nothing quite like this...

She's fighting for her freedom but when her strongest ally is found murdered, everything is on the line—including her own life.

With her rag-tag band of supernatural friends in tow, Holly's off to launch her biggest—and most dangerous—investigation yet. She must stop the killer without setting off the SPA's alarms or else she can kiss her chance at freedom goodbye.

CHAPTER 1

It's strange how a place can change so much and yet look exactly the same.

The last time I'd stepped foot inside the Seattle haven, the secret community hidden somewhere between the human and supernatural worlds, it was the place I called home. Now, standing on the main street that wound through the heart of the city, I felt like a complete stranger.

During my year of banishment, I'd grown detached from my old life inside the busy city. Magic pulsed through the haven, an undercurrent of all the powerful forces and beings that walked the glittering streets. In the past, that swirl of power would have excited me. Now it was overwhelming and confusing.

Then again, the reason for my trek to my former home wasn't exactly cause for celebration and undoubtedly added to my anxiety. In less than twenty-four hours I'd be standing before the powerful Haven Council, waiting to see if I would ever be allowed to practice potion magic again. My lawyer was confident, but his assurance hadn't quite yet rubbed off on me. My world was spinning as though I'd just stepped off a merry-go-round that had been going a hundred miles an hour.

However, I was determined to ignore the urge to hurl long enough to have lunch with one of my longtime friends —and paranormal party-planning extraordinaire—Anastasia Winters. So after stopping off at my city central hotel long enough to drop off my cat, Boots, and get him settled with a bowl of kibble, I headed out to meet Anastasia at Finnegan's, one of the haven's best cafes. Their claim to fame was the hearty soups they prepared and served in miniature cauldrons. Old-world style. All the charm, none of the barbaric treatment. Not to mention their cherry cider was the best thing to ever come out of a barrel.

Walking the streets of the haven was a surreal experience. All of the shops and restaurants I used to frequent were bustling with witches and wizards, shifters, werecreatures, and goblins. I even spotted a majestic centaur striding down the street. The farther I walked, the more comfortable I became. My anxiety ebbed and I actually started to smile as I drank it all in—the sights, the sounds, the smells. Beechwood Harbor was populated with supernaturals. I was hardly alone. But there was something about being immersed in it. The freedom of not having to hide what I was. I could let my witch-flag fly high and proud. I could send up a shower of pink and gold sparks that would rain down as glittering butterflies and no one would bat an eye.

Still smiling, I turned the corner and veered away from the main street through the haven's mercantile district to a small cluster of shops. Finnegan's was wedged between a handcrafted potion shop I used to frequent and a bookstore that sold enchanted books that read aloud as the pages were flipped. I had quite a collection of them, as they proved to be handy tools to have while doing potion work that required getting a little messy. For some reason, that seemed to apply to most of the ones I made.

I stopped short when I rounded the corner. The potion shop was gone, the windows boarded up and dark. I moved closer but didn't see any signs the building was for sale or lease. I cupped my hands and peered inside the dirt-caked windows. The shop appeared dank and grimy, as though no one had been there in quite some time. My heart sank at what the once charming and vibrant shop had been reduced to. I also wondered what had happened to Mrs. Clairmont, the owner of the shop. She'd been a widow for nearly a decade, and always kept the shop stocked with carefully crafted homemade potions. She'd run the place single-handedly but never hesitated to stop and answer my questions when I was first learning the process of making custom potions. I hadn't thought about her in quite some time but suddenly missed her as I stared inside her abandoned shop.

"Holly!"

I whirled around at Anastasia's voice and saw the pretty brunette running delicately in her impossibly high stiletto boots. I liked nice shoes as much as the next witch, but I honestly had no idea how Anastasia made it through the day without breaking both of her ankles.

She leapt up onto the sidewalk and grabbed me in a tight embrace. "I can't believe you're here!" she said into my long auburn hair as it whipped through the wind.

I smiled. "And I didn't even have to wear a disguise."

She laughed, the sound melodic like a tinkling wind chime. When she pulled away, she kept her hands on my arms. We'd spoken on the phone many times since my banishment and met for lunch a couple of times in Seattle proper, but the visits had been few and far between. Seattle was over three hours away from Beechwood Harbor, so visits usually involved a long train ride and a hotel room for the night. Anastasia had officially moved inside the haven following her big promotion at work and my banishment prevented me from staying on her pull-out couch. At first, I'd tried to use my Larkspur necklace but found—after several uncomfortable attempts—that it only allowed me to jump short distances.

"How are you?" Anastasia asked, finally releasing me. "How does it feel to be back?"

"It's kind of weird," I replied. "In Beechwood Harbor, there's a certain charge in the air, I think from the ocean. My magic responds to it. But here, all the magic energy feels like a collision. I'm not used to it anymore."

Anastasia flapped a hand. "I'm sure you'll settle right back in!"

"Well I don't know if I should get too comfortable. After all, I'm not sure how long I'll be allowed to stay." Reminded of the vacant potion shop, I craned around and hitched my thumb. "Although that's new. What happened?"

Anastasia looked troubled and she linked her arm through mine. "Come on, let's go order some lunch. It's freezing out here. You'd think with all the magic housed within this haven, we could at least work out how to keep the weather at a stable seventy-five!"

I frowned at her sudden change of topic but let her steer me through Finnegan's doors. The owner, Walter Finnegan, greeted us warmly and, for a moment, I forgot all about the shop next door. We were promptly seated at a table with a window and, without consulting the menu, ordered two huge cauldrons of soup. While we waited, the owner brought out a still-steaming loaf of bread with a thick crust, and we both dug in.

"Tell me about work. Still loving it?" I asked, unsure if I should ask about Mrs. Clairmont's shop again.

Anastasia nodded, her mouth full of bread.

I smiled and dragged my chunk through the basil-infused olive oil. "That's good to hear."

She wiped her fingers off on a linen napkin and then dabbed at her mouth. "It's been wonderful so far. Planning weddings, especially ones where I can kind of go a little crazy with magic, is so much more fun than birthday parties and retirement shindigs."

I laughed. "I'll bet."

"My calendar is booked for the next eighteen months. Solid!" A wide smile crossed her face as she leaned in slightly. "However, I could definitely squeeze you and Adam in …"

I choked on a mouthful of bread and quickly reached for my water glass. Shaking my head vigorously, I replied, "No chance of that. At least, not in that time frame!"

Anastasia pursed her lips. "Why not? I could do *so* much with your big day!"

I smiled politely. "Stace, I hate to break it to you, but that's not a *super* convincing reason to rush into marriage."

"Why not?"

I arched a brow. "Are you serious? You actually need me to spell that argument out for you?"

She held her pout for another moment and then waved it off with a flick of her wrist "Fine, fine. But I reserve the right to at least a six-month lead-up *when* it happens."

When was more like *if*, but I wasn't going to argue semantics with her over lunch.

Walter personally brought out our meals and I smiled gratefully, both for the soup and the timely interruption. Once we assured him the food was to our liking, he bowed out and went back to the kitchen. The small dining room was full of late-lunch patrons and the steam from all the soup made the air thick and warm and filled with the scent of fresh bread and varied seasonings.

Anastasia stirred the contents of her cauldron and

glanced up at me. "Tell me about this meeting with the council. Are you nervous?"

I swallowed hard. "Nervous is an understatement."

Anastasia gave a sympathetic smile. "I can imagine. I had to go before the Haven Council once. It was years ago. A disgruntled client filed a complaint against A Touch of Magic and I had to go to provide testimony. It was … *intimidating*. To say the least."

"Teddy, my lawyer, says that as far as he can tell, the whole thing is more of a formality, but I think he might be glossing over the situation a little bit."

"Why's that?" Anastasia asked, cocking her head slightly.

I drew in a deep breath. "Because of everything with Gabriel and the past. Teddy says that since my name was cleared years ago, it shouldn't be an issue, but you remember what happened right before Harvey shipped me off to Beechwood Harbor. I was in a jail cell faster than you could say *chocolate volcano centerpieces*."

"Not a bad idea. You mind if I jot that one down?" Anastasia teased. "It could be a riskier version of a fondue pot."

I smiled and scooped up another bite of my soup. "Obvious I hope I'm wrong, but I think Teddy might have a tougher fight than he's prepared for. He's from the Los Angeles haven and has a solid practice there. And sure, maybe some of the council members here have heard of him, but I don't think that's going to matter very much when it comes right down to it. There's a bias that follows me around and I'm not sure they will be willing to hand over a pardon just because I have a flashy, out-of-town lawyer."

"Didn't you say your SPA agent is testifying on your behalf? That's gotta carry some weight."

I nodded. "Harvey promised to be there. I helped him with a case a few weeks back but he's definitely the wild card factor."

Anastasia frowned. "I'm sorry this has been such a mess for you, Holly. I can't even imagine."

"Thanks." I shrugged and took another bite, savoring the blend of spices. "Worst case scenario, I'll at least be able to come and go from the haven. But if I can't open my potions business again, I'm not sure how much good that will do me."

"And if you get your license, or at least the chance to apply for one, will you move back? What about Adam?"

"I don't know yet. We haven't really talked about it."

She furrowed her brows. "What would you want?"

"There are things I've missed about haven life," I replied with another glance around the cafe and the occupants of the other tables. "But I have a feeling that if I moved back, I might actually miss Beechwood Harbor even more."

Anastasia gave a sad smile. I wondered if she'd already been expecting that answer. "I won't beg you to move back, but I will require that you visit more. Especially since you'll be able to stay with me in my condo!"

"Definitely! I'll be happy to be able to shop for potion ingredients in person instead of over the Witches Web. There's just no replacing the in-person experience when you're picking out the right fekir salve or pickled silk worms."

"Lovely." Anastasia's face went a little green as she considered her next bite. "Call me crazy, Holly, but I think I'll stick to shoe shopping."

I laughed and broke off another piece of bread. "Fair enough."

We finished our lunches and after Anastasia out-wrestled me for the check, we headed out of Finnegan's. We stopped at the edge of the sidewalk to bundle back into our coats and I glanced at the abandoned shop next door. I gestured toward the blackened windows again. "So what happened? Is Mrs. Clairmont all right?"

Anastasia sighed. "I don't want to worry you, but this kind of thing has been happening a lot lately. Smaller shops are closing down while new chains move into the area. The chain stores charge half what Mrs. Clairmont used to. Personally, I think the charms and potions are a little weak, and forget it if you need something custom, but the supers around here seem to gobble it up."

I shook my head. "Don't they realize the kind of ingredients that go into those *fast food* potions?"

"If they do, they don't seem to care. The Jewelbox Apothecary has been stocking more custom potions lately. Maybe Mrs. Clairmont has been selling hers there. Do you want to swing by on the way back to your hotel?"

I shook my head. "No, that's all right. The last thing I need to be worrying about is the future of the potion-making market right now." I brightened a little and glanced down the street in the opposite direction. "You know what I do need though..."

Anastasia grinned. "Don't tell me you're *still* obsessed with Lemon Clouds?"

I laughed and looped my arm through hers. "Hey, I haven't had a fresh one in over a year. Humor me."

After I stocked up on all manner of sweets and treats at my favorite bakery, Anastasia walked with me back to my hotel. The three-level building had a brick facade with lush greenery that framed the wide stairs that led to the front doors. I glanced up toward the room I'd checked into a couple of hours earlier. The room was sandwiched on the second floor and had a view of the street. I smiled when I spotted a fuzzy, orange backside pressed up against the glass. Clearly Boots was making the most of the last bit of sunlight breaking through the gray clouds.

"Holly!"

I turned and caught sight of Teddy as he jogged across the

busy street, one hand raised in greeting, the other clutching the handle of a leather briefcase.

"Teddy! Hello."

His blonde hair flapped in the breeze and his usually rosy cheeks had even more color from the chill of the late-winter afternoon. "Did you just arrive?" he asked when he came to a stop.

I shook my head. "I checked in a little while ago. Teddy, this is Anastasia Winters. We're old friends. Stacy, this is Teddy, my lawyer."

Anastasia smiled warmly as they shook hands. "Nice to meet you."

"Likewise."

She eyed Teddy skeptically. "I hope you're the shark Holly's been promised."

"I don't know about that." Teddy chuckled. "Besides, I don't think she's going to have much need for a shark. Things seem to be pretty cut and dried at this point. I can't see one reason why they would bar her from obtaining her license."

Anastasia smiled but I knew that, like me, she had her doubts it would be that easy. "I suppose we'll find out tomorrow, right?"

Teddy nodded and shifted the case from one hand to the other. "Hopefully that's all it will take, but if they ask for further information, it could potentially take a little longer."

After an uncomfortable pause, Stacy smiled and nodded. "Well I wish you both luck! Teddy, it was nice to meet you. Please, take care of my dear Holly."

Teddy gave a winning smile and brushed a hand on my arm as he started up the front steps of the hotel. "I'll get checked in. Holly, please let me know when you have a minute so we can go over some last minute details."

"Of course."

He waved and then disappeared inside.

"He seems nice," Anastasia said once the door flapped closed again. "He doesn't quite fit the image I had in mind though. He looks very young."

"Well, that's LA for you. In any case, Evangeline speaks highly of him and I trust her judgment."

Anastasia embraced me. "I'm sure it will all work out. Like he said, it should be open and shut."

"Thanks, Stacy."

Smiling, she pulled away and squeezed my shoulders. "Call me before you head out of town, all right?"

"I will. Thanks for lunch."

"Anytime."

Anastasia waved her hand and a sleek black car pulled up at the curb. She'd given up having her own car when she moved from Seattle proper into the haven. She was within walking distance to her office and said there was no need to pay the absurd parking fees when there was a plethora of cabs within the haven.

As soon as her cab was out of sight, I released a heavy sigh and headed to the front entrance of the hotel. The afternoon with Anastasia had served as a wonderful distraction from the real purpose behind my visit to the haven, but in her absence, all of my underlying anxiety rushed back like a tidal wave.

CHAPTER 2

The hotel lobby was warm and smelled faintly like cookies. On my way to the elevator, I noticed a group of men and women, most dressed in business suits, gathered around a slate-tiled fireplace. Upstairs, I bypassed my own room and went straight to Teddy's to see if he had news that would help ease my building sense of panic. He'd booked two separate rooms for our stay and the hotel had put them together near the end of the second-floor hallway. I walked to his door and raised a hand to knock but paused, smiling as the sound of his voice filtered through. He was singing an upbeat song that I recognized but couldn't quite place. It hit me half a second later; the song was one by the popular witch pop singer, Petra. I stifled a laugh as I rapped on his door. Petra's fan base usually leaned toward a younger crowd and the image of Teddy in his signature three-piece suit singing along with a crowd of teenagers cracked me up. The singing stopped abruptly and I laughed a little harder when I imagined Teddy's panicked expression on the other side, wondering if I'd heard him.

The door flew open a moment later and a blushing Teddy

smiled sheepishly as he granted me entrance. "Hello Holly. I hope I didn't cut your meeting short."

Still smiling, I stepped inside and glanced around his room. It was a mirrored layout of my own room. A living space, kitchenette, and round table with four chairs took up the majority of the suite. A short hallway led to the single bedroom and small powder room. The bedroom had its own en suite bathroom, which I could get used to, not that Posy would ever allow construction within the Beechwood Manor. If anyone ever tried, she'd probably round up a ghost posse and haunt the general contractor into an early retirement.

"Is your room satisfactory?" Teddy asked, moving to the wet bar where he'd clearly been mixing up a drink.

"It's perfect. Overkill, actually." I smiled at him and wound my tangled mess of hair into a ponytail. The wind had done a number on my long tresses. For some reason, just being around Teddy drove me to fidget with my hair or clothing. In his manicured and polished shadow, it was hard not to feel grubby. "You really didn't have to book suites. I would have been fine on the fold-out couch at Stacy's house."

Teddy frowned at me over his shoulder. "A fold-out couch?"

I shrugged.

Evangeline, my witch roommate and good friend, had insisted on paying Teddy's fee on my behalf, so while I didn't personally know how much he made per hour, it was obvious Teddy was an extremely wealthy wizard. Judging by the way he dressed and carried himself, he'd never known what it was like to *want* for anything.

Evangeline had met Teddy while she was living in the Los Angeles haven, working as the high-profile star of a paranormal soap opera. Since relocating to Beechwood Harbor, she had toned down her own lifestyle—although I still had yet to see her wear the same outfit twice—but Teddy was still full-blown LA and looked ready to simultaneously walk a runway and commandeer a boardroom.

"Can I pour you a drink?" Teddy asked me.

"Sparkling water with lime, please. I indulged in a few glasses of spiked cherry cider at lunch and should probably quit while I'm ahead."

"Coming right up," Teddy chuckled. "Please sit."

I took the chair he indicated and crossed my legs. He carried the drinks over, handed one to me, and then skirted the marble-topped coffee table to take a seat on the opposite couch. "Thank you."

Teddy inclined his head and then proceeded to assess me over the rim of his crystal tumbler. "How are you feeling?"

My fingers twisted together in my lap, warring with one another just as much as the thoughts in my head. "All right, I guess. It's good to be back in the haven."

Teddy nodded. "I haven't been to this haven in some time, but I could see myself getting used to it."

I arched an eyebrow, but then a slow smile spread across my face. "Are you planning more frequent visits?"

Teddy's ruddy cheeks darkened as he dipped his chin.

"Are you and Evangeline—?"

Teddy glanced up and then shook his head. "Evangeline is like a butterfly. She flits from place to place."

Or from man to man. Actually, more accurately, from wizard to shifter and then back again. Evangeline liked to flirt and be admired. I wasn't entirely sure she intended to ever settle down. But, in my opinion, a man like Teddy would be a good fit for her personality. He was stable, dependable, and had the style and polish that matched well with Evangeline's exotic beauty.

"In any case, that's a topic for another day. For now, let's talk about tomorrow," he said, effortlessly brushing aside the uncomfortable conversation. He set his tumbler on the coffee table and then went to the table near the kitchen. He opened the case I'd seen him carrying outside and retrieved the enchanted notepad he'd used during all our previous meetings. His pen transcribed notes during all of his business conversations. Thanks to some enchantment, the words were written as they were spoken, only to immediately disappear from the page. I wasn't sure how he retrieved the notes, as the pages were blank slates as soon as the conversation ended. It was certainly a secure way of handling his sensitive business, even if it was more than a little mysterious.

"During the flight from LA, I went back through our previous conversations and have a few last-minute questions," he said, taking his seat again. He placed the notepad on the table and the pen went to work, moving as if an invisible hand were scribbling furiously as Teddy continued. "I know you worked in a potion shop at one time, but when I was building the case notes, I looked it up and couldn't find a record of you ever having applied for a license before."

"That's right. My previous boss wouldn't sign off on any of the apprentice tasks. He barely let me *touch* potion supplies."

Teddy's brows furrowed together. "What were you doing then?"

"Sweeping, mostly."

Teddy nodded slowly, as though trying to fit jigsaw puzzle pieces together. "What was his reasoning? As an apprentice, you should have been working under his supervision, not doing page work."

"I know." I sighed as I sagged back against the chair like a deflated balloon. "Because of my association with Gabriel and the ring of dark wizards, most shops wouldn't even let me fill out an application. Mr. Keel was the only one who gave me a job and that was mostly because one of my friends from my academy days is his niece and begged him to hire me. I figured it would take some time to gain his trust, but if I ever gained any ground, I'll never know. I wasn't there all that long before the whole banishment thing happened."

I nearly laughed at how flippantly the words sounded. That whole *banishment thing* had dictated my life for the past year. At first I'd railed against it and cursed Harvey for giving the order, but after a year in Beechwood Harbor, I found it harder and harder to remain angry about it.

The council hearing wasn't even about the banishment order; Harvey had made it clear that his order was unofficial, and would only be put in my record if I broke the terms of his deal. The council hearing was to gain permission to apply for my potions license after a series of unfortunate events made it look as though I'd tried to smuggle a dangerous potion to my ex-boyfriend and haven anarchist, Gabriel Willows. Which, of course, was completely ridiculous. I was more than content to let Gabriel rot in an SPA prison for what he'd tried to do and even more so for the way he'd tangled me up in his scheming.

That was a web I was still trying to get out of. All I could do was hope this would be my final obstacle to living free and clear of the SPA.

Teddy reached for his drink. "I've spoken to Mr. Colepepper and he's assured me that he will, in fact, be present tomorrow at the hearing and will give testimony on your behalf if called forth by the council."

"I can't believe this is all really happening," I said, the words nearly a whisper. I'd never been before the council before. The entire idea was surreal. My life had reached a tipping point and everything could change all over again within the course of the next few days.

"Believe it, Holly. We'll have you back at the cauldron in

no time!" Teddy smiled and snapped his fingers. The pen stilled and then slowly dropped down to rest on the notepad. The last words sunk into the glossy surface and melted like candle wax until the page was blank again, not even a trace of pressure scratched into the thick paper. "Do you have any last questions for me?"

I swallowed hard. There was *one* question in my mind that I hadn't voiced to anyone.

I drew in a deep breath, gathering the strength to finally utter it. "What if they turn me down?" I asked with a cringe. "What if they refuse to give me a potions license or even the opportunity to properly apprentice and apply a year from now? What am I supposed to do then?"

It wasn't a question Teddy could really answer with any surety. Although, to his credit, he tried. He leaned forward, hands clasped together, and said, "I don't think you have to worry about that, Holly. I've tried a lot of cases and I see absolutely no room for this thing to go sideways. However, *if* things don't work, we have the right to petition for a second hearing."

I nodded slowly. I appreciated his confidence, but I couldn't quite wrap myself up in it, at least not fully. I missed potion work more than I'd ever expected. It was more than a profession or trade. It was part of my being, my identity. To have it taken away was like having a part of my heart go missing. It wasn't about the lost customers—although that was a concern too—or the whispers within the supernatural community in Beechwood Harbor. It was far bigger than that.

Teddy pushed to his feet and I followed his lead. "I'll come collect you in the morning. Try to get some sleep."

"Thank you, Teddy. For everything," I replied, not bothering to point out the unlikeliness of sleep.

Now, if I could whip up a sleeping potion, it would be a different story.

~

Teddy knocked on my door bright and early the following morning. As expected, the night had stretched on painstakingly hour by hour without the relief of sleep. Even Boots was restless and moody. Of course, that could easily be remedied with a bowl of tuna fish. My problems weren't quite as easy to solve.

After saying goodbye to Boots, I followed Teddy out of the hotel and into a waiting sedan. Neither of us said much on the ride to the council hall. He started to ask about my night, but stopped when he saw the expression on my face.

Harvey Colepepper was waiting for us in the hallway outside the appointed court room. I'd seen Harvey in a suit before, but seeing him standing there on the steps all dressed up and knowing it was for my benefit warmed my heart. We'd had our ups and downs—mostly downs—but that was in the past. He wore his usual grim expression as we approached. "Holly. Teddy," he said, nodding up at each of us.

Harvey was a goblin hybrid and stood no higher than my hip, even shorter when compared to Teddy, who had a few inches on me. But Harvey carried himself in a way that made his stature easy to forget.

"Hello, Harvey," I said. "Thank you for coming today. It really means a lot."

"A deal is a deal," was all he said.

A pall hung in the air, as though we were meeting at a funeral instead of a council hearing.

I watched Harvey out of the corner of my eye as we entered the council hall. Did he know something I didn't?

A large wooden clock occupied the majority of the wall above the reception desk, where a team of exhausted-looking clerks worked to herd and direct the incoming lines of people. I was surprised by the amount of activity. Had the Seattle haven become such a chaotic place that there was the need for that many people coming and going from the main legal building?

Harvey, as though sensing my question, said, "There is a high profile case being held this week in the grand hall."

Teddy glanced down at him. "The Praxle case, right?"

"Praxle?" I asked when Harvey nodded. "What is that?"

"Don't you watch *The Witch Wire*?" Harvey asked me with a sharp look.

"What can I say? After a year of *banishment* I've fallen out of the habit of watching *Witch Wire* every night."

Harvey bristled and tugged at the lapels of his jacket.

Teddy stepped in. "Bill Praxle is a business man who owns a chain of variety shops throughout West Coast havens. He's being tried on charges related to his questionable business practices."

"What does that even mean?" I asked, not bothering to look at Harvey.

"There are quite a few charges. The catalyst, and reason why the council hearing is happening here in the Seattle haven, is that a witch who ran a potion shop was bullied into selling her shop. She claims she was threatened and even assaulted by a hired mercenary before finally agreeing to sell to Mr. Praxle."

"Wait—was that witch Mrs. Clairmont?" I asked, suddenly realizing Praxle must be the man behind the chain of shops Anastasia had told me about the day before.

Harvey nodded. "Yes. At her urging, we launched a full investigation and came up with half a dozen other victims. The hearing started a few days ago and it's attracted the attention of the media."

He didn't sound particularly happy about that part. As one of the key figures in the crimes division of the Seattle branch of the SPA, it had no doubt buried him in a huge pile of red tape.

I glanced at Harvey, noting the tightness in his expression. Guilt surged through me when I realized he was spending valuable time with me instead of on such an important case. I reached out and brushed his shoulder. "I'm sorry for snapping at you, Harvey. I'm just edgy."

We'd had our differences—a mountain of them—but somewhere along the way, I'd moved beyond the anger I'd felt toward him after initially being banished and, most recently, when he'd dragged me from the manor in handcuffs right as Adam's parents had arrived for Yule Feast. Not the shining meet-the-parents moment I'd been hoping for.

As infuriating as I found Harvey's ever-present involvement in my life, I could now see that he truly did have good intentions in his little goblin-hybrid heart. The realization smacked me in the face now that he was minutes away from testifying on my behalf to help me get me my life back.

It's the little things.

"Will Mrs. Clairmont get her potion shop back when this is over?" I asked them as another stream of chattering reporters made their way through the doors.

"I doubt it," Harvey said with his signature flatness as he turned his back on the scene. "She took a crippling financial hit fighting Mr. Praxle before smaller councils for years prior to his escalation in tactics. I don't think she has the means to get back into business."

My heart twisted. "That's awful."

The door to the courtroom opened and a man in a dark suit stepped out into the hall and gave each of us a seething look. Magic pulsed from him, palpable and strong. A blue-and-white badge was clipped to the pocket on his jacket, identifying him as an officer of the council. Basically a glorified bouncer with an extra dose of legal firepower behind his authority. "Case number?" he said, his words clipped.

Teddy pulled out a paper with the Haven Council's letterhead at the top and the guard flicked his hand. A blue pulse of magic swept down the page and then returned to his palm. "The council will see you now. Step forward one at a time and wait for the scan to complete before proceeding."

I gave a nervous nod and watched as Teddy went first. He held out his arms, as though being frisked at a checkpoint, and that same wave of ice blue enveloped him before returning to the guard. Harvey flashed his official SPA badge and was spared the scanning process.

I cast an anxious glance at Teddy as I put my arms out and waited. "You ready?" he asked, concern etched in his brow.

Was it too late to say no?

CHAPTER 3

The bright light from the hallway was immediately snuffed out as the hulking guard pulled the door closed behind me. I stumbled forward into the dimly lit chamber and gawked at the room. It was a stark contrast to the bright hallway we'd been waiting in. If the designers had been going for medieval chic, they'd nailed it. Teddy and Harvey both looked comfortable, barely noticing their surroundings as they led the way to the front of the room. Harvey veered off to the left and gingerly took a seat on one of eight wooden benches that lined each side of the central aisle. Teddy continued, not stopping until he reached the long table at the front of the room. The guard disappeared behind a side door and I scurried to Teddy's side. The room was quiet. *Too* quiet. Every sound any of us made seemed to echo through the expansive room.

Iron chandeliers hung from the ceiling, three over the council table alone, but it still didn't feel like enough light.

"Holly, it's all right," Teddy whispered out of the corner of his mouth. "Try to relax. Deep breaths."

I sucked in a shallow breath. It wasn't like me to get

rattled. In the last year alone I'd gone head to head with a nasty gargoyle, a chilling, remorseless sociopath, and a pack of power-hungry vampires. A board of crusty old witches and wizards who served as council members shouldn't bring me to the point of a meltdown. All the same, I couldn't quite manage to get enough air.

The guard reappeared followed by six robed figures. Teddy shot to his feet, dragging me up with him. Out of the corner of my eye, I saw Harvey hop down from his seat on the bench to stand. The council members filed quietly to their seats at the long, elevated desk across the room and took their seats. "The high and honorable Haven Council will now hear case number 45268b."

The guard turned about-face and stood like a sentry at the side of the desk. I worked down the line, examining each face. There were three wizards and three witches. Other types of supernaturals were able to hold places within the SPA and other areas of law enforcement but were prohibited from actually serving as council members. It was controversial within the havens system. An old—some would say archaic—law.

None of the six faces staring at me seemed particularly friendly. They were mostly older with white or graying hair, with the exception of the woman at the very end of the table. She looked to be closer to my age, with long, dark curls, a porcelain complexion, and piercing eyes that reminded me of Flurry, Evangeline's falcon familiar. While the others looked at their notes, she kept those dark eyes locked on mine without blinking. A shiver ran down my spine.

The wizard in the middle cleared his throat and all eyes swiveled toward him. "Holly Boldt, according to your petition, you are present before the council to waive your apprenticeship requirements and acquire your master potions license. Is this correct?"

"Yes, uh, your honor?"

Teddy frowned. Apparently I'd been watching too many human cop shows. "Ms. Boldt is indeed here to pursue her master potions license, a right that was unjustly stripped from her one year ago after a series of misunderstandings."

The council members all snapped to attention and stared at Teddy. He remained cool, his expression firm but not aggressive. "And you are?" the wizard in the center spat at Teddy.

"Theodore Trevail, a member of the Los Angeles Haven Justice Department. I am here to present Ms. Boldt's case."

None of the council members seemed too impressed with Teddy's credentials. In fact, all six of them looked like they'd collectively swallowed a lemon.

"Well," the young witch at the end started, her voice a sickly sweet purr. "As impressed as I'm sure we all are, this case seems quite straightforward based on what we've reviewed in the file. Ms. Boldt was arrested in connection to Gabriel Willows circle. I'm sure no one present needs be to reminded just what that particular merry band of misfits was up to." She smiled at her fellow council members.

Teddy bristled beside me and the flicker of hope inside my chest start to sputter. "Ms. Boldt was cleared of any connection to the ring's violent plans or the dark magic they were harnessing. She was an innocent bystander, mistakenly lumped in with a dangerous group—an accident that has been remedied."

The young witch scoffed. "An *accident*? That's your best defense?" she asked, her dark eyes boring into me.

I straightened, pulling my shoulders back. "The charges were dropped. Besides that, I'm not on trial. Am I?"

Teddy flexed his jaw and held up a hand. "Ms. Boldt is correct. This petition has nothing to do with those unfortunate events of the past. She is here, as a citizen of the Seattle haven, to petition for her right to acquire her master potions license."

The witch tossed her dark hair over her shoulder and smiled. "I'm not sure how you expect us to untangle the two things. If Ms. Boldt shares these ideologies, the last thing this council wants to do is allow her access to dangerous—and potentially dark—magic. In any form."

I sighed. I should have known it would come down to the past. I cast a glance at Harvey, hoping he could swoop in and argue on my behalf. He'd promised to testify to my intentions as well as my skill level as a potion witch. To my dismay, he remained seated, his long fingers folded together in his lap, and even though I knew he must have felt my gaze on him, he refused to look my way.

"There are no charges against her. No evidence linking her to Willow's circle," Teddy stressed.

"Then why do I see that she was arrested again in connection to the group, even after Mr. Willows was in an SPA prison?" the witch asked, her teeth flashing like a victorious wolf about to devour a meal. "In fact, it looks like following that arrest, she was *banished* from all of haven society. Yet we are supposed to believe she is harmless? Her own assigned SPA agent ordered her unfit for haven life."

My eyes flashed to Harvey. That arrest was supposed to have been scrubbed from my record. How in the Otherworld had the council ended up with that information? Had Harvey betrayed me?

Harvey still refused to meet my eyes and I bit back the urge to shout his name.

Teddy tensed his jaw. "She was *questioned* in regard to a situation. That is not the same as an arrest. As to the banishment, that was a temporary—and unofficial—order that bears no weight in this hearing."

The witch clasped her slender fingers together and rested

them on the table. "Perhaps I need to put this in other terms, seeing as how Ms. Boldt has been living among the *humans* for such a long time. Let's see … how does that expression go? Ah, yes, where there's smoke, there's fire. And simply put, Ms. Boldt, there is simply too much smoke hovering over your head for this council to feel it wise to grant you permission to attain a potions master license that would enable you to sell your creations within the havens. In fact, I'm not sure why we aren't making this banishment a permanent order. It certainly seems to be working. The Willows gang hasn't so much as crossed my radar in the past year you've been gone." She cast a sidelong glance at the other council members, who silently confirmed her statement.

Anger and despair surged up inside me and clashed together in an explosion of emotion. Tears sprang to my eyes even as my hands fisted into tight balls at my sides. "This is outrageous!" I cried. "Why am I being punished for things I didn't do?"

Teddy reached out and grasped my forearm. "Holly, please," he whispered. I slammed my mouth shut and ground my teeth as he turned back to address the council. "At this time, to clear up the issue of the banishment, I would like to call for a testimony. An esteemed member of the SPA and Ms. Boldt's assigned agent, Harvey Colepepper."

Teddy turned, waving a hand to present our key witness, only to find the bench empty.

Harvey was gone.

"No," the plea, a whisper, slipped from my lips.

"Guess he had something else to do?" the young witch cooed.

I stared, transfixed, at the empty bench as the wizard who'd started the proceedings asked Teddy if there was anything else.

"Ms. Boldt is a noble witch who has worked to move past

the stigma that is inexplicably still clinging to her following the unfortunate events cited here today. She's followed the law of the haven to the letter and deserves to use her natural gifts to not only provide a living for herself, but to also help other supernaturals inside the haven community as well as outside. I would ask that the council consider this issue thoroughly before dismissing it based on loose, circumstantial footnotes in her case files. As to the banishment, Mr. Colepepper never intended that to be a permanent order and I am confident he will clear up any concerns just as soon as he is available."

The council members looked from Teddy to me. They hadn't proclaimed their final decision yet, but I knew it was over all the same.

My eyes slid closed. I drew in a long, slow breath and willed the room to stop spinning.

"We will call you forth when we have had a chance to examine the evidence. Please, Reginald, escort Mr. Trevail and Ms. Boldt from the chamber."

The stocky guard swept forward and ushered us back to the hall. When the door closed, Teddy ripped his phone from the pocket of his jacket and furiously dialed. "Where in the Otherworld is that little *troll*? Someone better be bleeding."

I didn't bother correcting him as to Harvey's species. I was too busy cooking up insults of my own to hurl at him when he was back in my sights. Why had he bothered to make me promises, show up for the hearing, and then vanish midway through? On top of that, somehow the council had gotten their hands on the files he supposedly buried. That was the arrangement we'd made. Well, that he'd made and forced me to agree to. He'd promised to erase as long as I went peacefully to Beechwood Harbor and never stepped foot back inside the Seattle haven. If he hadn't tipped off the council, then who had?

Teddy snapped his phone shut. "His calls are going to his assistant, Harriet. She claims she doesn't know where he is."

I sighed deeply and dropped my head back to rest on the cool wall behind me. "I'm sorry I wasted your time, Teddy."

Teddy softened and sat beside me. "It's not your fault, Holly. Harvey is the one who should be apologizing. I didn't quite expect the council to put so much weight on the past seeing as how none of the charges stuck. But even still, one word from Harvey and this all could have been cleared away."

I nodded. "I don't know what I expected to happen here today but I thought they would at least *listen*. At first, it seemed like it, but then that woman. That witch. Who is she?"

Teddy shook his head. "I don't know. I'm not familiar with the Seattle branch of the council. My guess? She's some youngblood who was added to the council so they didn't have to cancel the proceedings. See, most of the higher-up council members are tangled up in this Praxle mess." He gestured across the expansive lobby. The crowds were dispelled now, but I remembered what Harvey and Teddy had said about it before our case was called. "She's obviously trying to make an impression."

"Well she certainly managed that," I deadpanned. "She blew a giant hole right through my entire case."

Teddy pushed up from the bench. "Wait here; I'll be right back."

He didn't wait for me to agree before scurrying off around the corner.

"Great," I said, heaving a sigh. "Even better. Total abandonment."

All I wanted to do was go back to my hotel room, grab a bag of Lemon Clouds, bury myself under the covers with

Boots, and read a book. I'd go back to Beechwood Harbor in the morning and start over. Again.

Minutes ticked by as I waited alone outside the chamber's door. Teddy came back looking even more grim than when he'd left. "Harvey's still not answering. His voicemail message says he's out on official business, but who knows what that means."

"And without him?"

Teddy nodded and sat back down beside me. "I'm sorry, Holly. I truly thought this would be an open and closed case."

"It's not your fault, Teddy." I squeezed my eyes closed, desperate to hide the hot tears that were welling up. "Thanks for trying."

"Well hold on." He patted my shoulder. "It's not over yet."

"It sure seems like it. Especially if that witch has anything to say about it."

Before Teddy could assuage my fears, the door swung open and the same guard appeared. He jerked his chin in the direction of the doorway. "They've reached their final decision."

That was fast.

Teddy gulped.

I scanned the hall, looking for any sign Harvey was on his way back, but the corridor was empty in both directions. A final glance at the reception desk confirmed he wasn't going to make it. After a moment, I gave up and let Teddy usher me back into the chamber where the robed council members sat behind their table. As we walked in, I noticed most of them refused to meet my eyes. All except for one … the witch at the end offered a wide smile as we took our places at the smaller table.

The wizard who'd opened the proceedings cleared his throat. "Ms. Boldt, we've reviewed the notes in the case file and had a lengthy discussion in regard to your request.

Unfortunately, we've ruled against your petition. At this time, we cannot grant your request."

Teddy started to object but the wizard snapped his fingers and a red ribbon, sparkling with magic, moved in a mesmerizing dance through the air and bound the petition as it rolled up like a scroll. When the bow formed, a hissing sound echoed through the chamber, signaling that the bond was permanent. Bonded. Final.

"This is outrageous!" Teddy shouted.

"Silence!" the wizard shouted, his voice booming like thunder. "The Haven Council has ruled. Reginald, see them out at once."

Reginald strode forward, his face set with determination. He pulled his wand as the council members stood and filed from the room until only the raven-haired witch remained. "Enjoy the human world, Holly," she purred before turning to follow her fellow council members from the room.

Only when the heavy wooden door shut behind them with a solid *thud* did I release a curse and a blast of magic that slammed into a chair, blowing it into a hundred splintered pieces.

Reginald let his own spell fly and I was thrown to the floor, my wrists instantly bound together. Teddy hurried forward and collected me, holding up a hand toward the guard. "Let her go."

"Out!" came Reginald's gruff reply. The spell released and I sprang from the floor like a boxer in the ring. Magic pulsed at my fingers, straining to be released, but Teddy wrapped one arm around my shoulder and steered me from the room before I had a chance to fire off another spell.

CHAPTER 4

"Are you going to be okay?"

Considering the circumstances we'd just walked away from, I found Teddy's question a little odd. I'd shrugged out of his reach and stalked out of the pristine building that housed the council and made it three blocks before I finally slowed enough that he'd managed to catch up. Thoughts raced through my mind faster than I could process them. Part of me wanted to sink down onto the curb and cry and the other part wanted to let out a blast powerful enough to rattle the entire haven and the city of Seattle that concealed it.

I stopped walking and spun on the heels of my black boots to face Teddy. Deep lines were etched around his eyes, erasing his boyish look, and I realized he was nearly as angry at the farce of a hearing as I was. "I'll be fine, Teddy. I'm sorry I lost control back there." I flapped a hand in the direction we'd come from.

"I understand," Teddy replied evenly. He slipped his hands deep in his pockets. "As soon as I get back to the hotel I'm going to file an appeal and a formal complaint."

I shook my head. "Don't bother."

"Holly, we can't give up."

My eyes drifted over his shoulder and followed the row of shops that lined the main street through the haven. The dull ache in my chest pounded as I drank it all in—the quaint shops with the shiny marquee signs that glittered and sparkled, each one competing for the attention of the supernatural patrons wandering the streets.

My gaze settled on a family as they wandered down the sidewalk. A blonde girl clung to her mother's and father's hands while a small white dog raced ahead of them. The fluffy pup stopped at the end of the sidewalk and suddenly shifted into a black cat. The blonde girl giggled and cheered. She slipped from her parent's grip and bounced in place, clapping her hands. The cat swished its tail and then transformed again, this time into a green lizard with a forked tongue. The girl darted back and grabbed her mother's leg. The father scooped her up and called out to the shapeshifter, who promptly turned into a small boy. The mother raced forward and wrapped a blanket around him because he'd shifted back to human form without clothing. She smiled at her son and scooped him into her arms as they continued down the street.

The ache grew sharper as I watched the small family. I dragged my eyes back to Teddy's. "I need some time."

Teddy gave a slight nod. "I'll walk you back to the hotel."

"No. That's all right. I know the way."

He frowned but didn't argue with me. I tried to smile but it fell flat. I hurried away, moving in the opposite direction as the little family of four. I couldn't watch them anymore.

Back in the hotel, Boots greeted me at the door with a series of yowls, only stopping when I gathered him into my arms. I squeezed him as tightly as I knew I could get away with and then set him down on the couch. As my familiar, he had the innate ability to pick up on my moods and emotions, and as his amber eyes shifted to follow me as I paced the suite, I could almost hear the question rolling around in his fuzzy little head.

"It didn't go so well, Bootsie. Looks like I'm going to have to come up with an alternate career plan."

His whiskers twitched.

"Don't worry," I said with a smile. "I'll find a way to buy your kibble."

My cell phone was on the small entryway table and I grabbed it up on my way back to the couch. I sat down beside Boots and he burrowed into my side. "Time to call Adam and tell him the news," I said with a heavy sigh. On the one hand, I desperately wanted to hear Adam's voice and have him tell me everything was going to turn out all right, but on the other, I dreaded rehashing all the details of the disastrous hearing.

He picked up after the second ring and sounded like he'd just finished running a mile. Considering it was barely noon, that wasn't likely. Adam liked to run through the woods behind the Beechwood Manor, but only after dark, when he could shift into his beast form and terrorize the forest as a shaggy dog that was more on par with the size of a grizzly bear than a canine. "Hey, gorgeous!" he panted into the phone. "I've been waiting to hear from you. How'd it go?"

"Are you all right?"

"Me? Uh—yeah, yeah. I'm good. Just been running around getting stuff done."

I frowned. "That sounds ... vague."

"Holls, come on, tell me what's going on."

I drew in a deep breath. "They denied my petition."

"What?" Adam boomed.

I yanked the phone away from my ear. "They dragged up everything with Gabriel and basically said I couldn't be trusted. They're even threatening to make my banishment permanent."

Adam swore.

"Yeah." I sighed and pressed my eyes closed. "It wasn't pretty."

"What about Harvey? Shouldn't his testimony or recommendation be enough?"

"He didn't testify."

"Why not? He's the one who convinced you to go before the council in the first place!"

"I don't know. SPA business. He disappeared in the middle of the hearing. In fact, I still haven't heard from him. Teddy found out he was called away but I don't know why or where."

"You think it was an excuse?"

I don't know yet. It doesn't make sense that he agreed to testify and help me if he had no intention of following through. Why lie about something like that? But then, there was one other thing that doesn't line up."

"Just one?" Adam said sarcastically. "To me, it sounds like the whole thing was messed up."

"The council had access to the files Harvey said were expunged. When he sent me to Beechwood Harbor, he told me he'd bury the report of the arrest and wouldn't report anything about the potions in my house as long as I left peacefully and didn't come back. He said it was for his own protection as much as mine."

"What do you suppose he meant by that?"

"I've always assumed he meant that he'd get in trouble if it ever came to light that I was illegally selling potions within the haven. As my agent, he was supposed to keep me out of trouble and he figured it would blow back on him if anybody found out that he let me go with a slap on the wrist."

"Banishment is hardly a slap on the wrist, gorgeous."

I nodded. He had a point. I'd never really had a chance to think about it much. I'd been too busy fitting into my new life at the manor and in the small, coastal town.

"There has to be something else going on," Adam continued.

"Well don't worry. Next time I see him, I'll be sure to ask him *all* about it."

Adam sighed. "I'm sorry the hearing didn't go well. What's the next step? I'm sure Teddy has a plan."

"He said he's going to file a complaint and an appeal. I'm not going to hold my breath, though."

"A complaint?"

"The hearing wasn't exactly by the book," I replied, my tone acidic. "They didn't listen to what either of us had to say and it was pretty obvious from the first minute that it wasn't going to go my way. There was one witch in particular who really got under my skin. It felt ... I don't know. It felt *personal* somehow. But I swear I have no idea who she is or why she would care so much whether or not I got my potions license."

"What's her name?"

"I don't know. They don't exactly wear nametags. Teddy is going to find out more. He said she's probably some kind of understudy trying to flaunt her newfound authority while the main council members are busy with this fraud case." I paused, remembering Mrs. Clairmont's shuttered potion shop. "When was the last time you were in the Seattle haven?"

"I don't know ... a few months ago, I guess. Most of my clients are humans and even when I'm in Seattle, I prefer to stay in a standard hotel and avoid all the hoopla."

I smiled. Adam was unapologetically himself, through and through. He'd left the haven system some years before and had no plan to ever return, despite his parents' insistence he needed to grow out of his "nomad" phase.

"Well, apparently this guy named Praxle has been pressuring businesses into selling to him so he can spread these chains of shops all over the haven. He was even having people hurt in order to scare them into giving up their property."

"Whoa. Fun guy."

I absently stroked Boots's fur. "Enough about this mess. Tell me what's going on at the manor. I've only been gone a couple of days and I already miss it."

"Well ...," Adam hesitated.

"What?" I asked, sitting up. "Is everything all right?"

"Mostly?"

"Not convincing."

Adam groaned. "I don't want to dump more problems on your shoulders, but things here aren't exactly going as planned either."

I scooted to the edge of the couch at the cringe in Adam's voice. Boots scowled up at me for disturbing him.

"What happened? Tell me you didn't get into it with Lacey." If he did, there was a fairly high likelihood the manor had paid the price. The owner—and resident ghost—Posy had a tendency to manifest her frustrations or anxieties into physical reactions through the house. With literal earth-shaking effects.

"No. No, this has nothing to do with Lacey. Other than the fact that we currently have a human living under the same roof as our favorite little undead princess and eventually she might want to swap out her faux blood smoothie for a hit of the real stuff."

"What? Who's at the manor?"

"Nick."

My brow furrowed. "Why?"

Nick Rivers owned a successful private investigation business and a beautiful one-bedroom condo on the outskirts of town. Why would he need to crash at the manor?

"I found him out in the bushes, prowling around last night."

"Sounds familiar," I said with a faint smile, recalling the first time Nick and I met.

"He's remembering things, Holly. About that night outside the Raven. He's asking too many questions and I don't know how to shut him up."

I winced. "Bat wings."

"Yeah. We've got to find a way to cast another memory-erasing spell before he brings us all down. From the sound of things, you can't really afford another scandal or to draw the eye of the council."

"Not particularly." I sighed. "Why was he prowling through the bushes?"

"He was looking for goblins. At least that's what he said. I figure he means Harvey."

"He remembers Harvey?" I yelped. "Bat wings! This is really bad, Adam."

"I know, Gorgeous. I talked him into coming inside and Evangeline slipped him some of your sleeping potion. I think she got the dose wrong though."

"Man alive," I groaned. "How much did she give him?"

"Two scoops?"

"Ugh. Why didn't you guys call me? At this rate, he's gonna be passed out until the weekend!"

"That might not be a bad thing," Adam said.

"Adam…"

"All right, all right. What's the antidote?"

I rambled off a recipe to bring Nick back from the land of the living dead and was about to wrap up the phone call when a loud thunk sounded through the wall of the adjoining suite. I frowned, wondering what Teddy was doing. Had he lost his temper and thrown something? I stood up and moved closer to the wall and heard another thud. This time, it sounded like a door being slammed. What in the Otherworld was he doing over there?

Seconds later, someone was pounding on the door to my suite. "Hold on a second, Adam." I went to the door and peered out through the peephole. Teddy was standing there, still beating on the door. I waved a hand, dispelling the security ward sealing the door, and pulled it open. Teddy's cheeks were drained of all their rosiness. His eyes were wide and a sheen of sweat coated his wide forehead. "Teddy? What's wrong?"

"Harvey's been ... Harvey's been found."

"Found?"

"Holly, he's—he's dead."

CHAPTER 5

*E*ven once I was seated on the couch, the room continued to spin. Teddy paced back and forth in front of me, speaking softly into the phone. My thoughts were jumbled and tangled to the point that I couldn't make sense of his conversation. Somewhere in my muddled thoughts, I realized I didn't even know who he was talking to. One panicked thought rang out above the rest: Harvey was gone, and if the gaping pit in my stomach was to be trusted, it had something to do with me.

Teddy stopped pacing. "All right. Call me when you hear something."

I looked up from the thick carpet of my hotel suite and met Teddy's eyes. "What happened?"

"I don't know many of the details yet." Teddy rubbed the back of his neck. "That was my contact in LA. He writes for the Haven Herald. He's looking into it, but someone found Harvey dead in the back seat of a taxi parked in the alley behind a warehouse in the industrial district."

"Of Seattle?"

Teddy nodded. "This is going to be tricky. The SPA has

called in their special task force that handles situations like this. They'll make sure the human who found him has his memory wiped and the cops don't interfere. They will set charms and wards over the scene to contain it until it's processed so humans won't see anything. We should have more information soon, but from what I'm hearing … it's not good." Teddy moved to take the armchair opposite my place on the couch. "Should you call back whomever you were talking to?"

I glanced at my cell phone. As soon as Teddy's news sunk in, I'd dropped it to the floor. Teddy had quickly swept it up and told the caller I'd get back to them and then hung up. "It was Adam."

Teddy gave a slight nod. "I assumed."

"I told him about the hearing and …" I squeezed my eyes closed as my words trailed off. "Stars, Teddy, I told him I thought Harvey had betrayed me."

Teddy leaned forward and grabbed one of my hands. "Holly, you can't beat yourself up. You didn't know. We *still* don't know what happened. I don't know what made Harvey leave the council chamber today. None of the pieces are fitting together right now. It's all speculation and what ifs. Let's wait to hear back from Marvin and then we'll figure out our next move."

"Okay." I gave Teddy's hand a gentle squeeze and stood up. "I'm going to call Adam back."

"I'll let you know if I hear anything else."

Teddy swept from the suite and went back to his room. I placed a new security ward on the door and then retrieved my phone and dialed Adam back with trembling fingers.

"Holly? What the heck happened to you? Are you all right?"

I nodded, trying to get myself under control and keep my

voice from wavering. "I'm fine but … Harvey was found. Adam, he's dead."

"What?" Adam sputtered.

"Teddy had been trying to reach him since the hearing. He just got word that Harvey was found dead in a taxi in some back alley inside Seattle proper."

"What happened? Was it a crash?"

"No, it wasn't a crash. We're waiting for more details. Apparently a human found him parked and called it into the Seattle police. The SPA is in the process of taking over the scene." I paused, fidgeting with the ends of my hair. "But I'm pretty sure I heard Teddy use the word gruesome."

"Where are you right now?" Adam asked. I could almost see him going for the stairs, hitting the entryway, and throwing on his leather jacket.

"I'm at the hotel."

"I'm leaving right now. I'll take a cab. The train takes too long." The background noises rose and fell as he verbally mapped out his plan.

"Adam," I said with a deep sigh. "I'm fine." I wished I sounded more convincing. Truth was, the whole thing had me rattled. It had been an extraordinarily odd day and in a few hours, the sun would be setting on a terrible tragedy.

"Holly, this is not up for debate. I'm coming. You shouldn't be alone with all this going on."

I rolled my eyes, but somewhere inside I was glad he would arrive before dark and I wouldn't have to spend what was likely to be a sleepless night alone. "All right. I'll call if I hear anything else."

We ended the call and I passed the time by taking a long shower. It was far from relaxing but at least the hot water beating down on my back helped ease the knotted muscles that felt as though they'd been bunched together for months, ever since Harvey had shown up at the manor and caught me making potions in the kitchen.

I sighed deeply and tried to sort through the lingering questions over his sudden disappearance from the hearing. Had he left over an SPA emergency? And if so, why hadn't his assistant known his whereabouts? Or had he left because he never had any intention of testifying on my behalf? Maybe he'd turned over the complete, unrestricted case files and hung me out to dry. Or was there another reason? Maybe he'd simply seen the writing on the wall and decided to get back to work. The council hadn't exactly appeared *open* to hearing another version of the story.

I stepped out of the shower and wrapped myself in the plush robe furnished by the hotel then knotted the sash and went into the adjoining bedroom and found my phone. Perched on the edge of the giant bed, I dialed Harvey's number. The call patched over to his assistant, who sounded muffled and subdued when she answered. "Harvey Colepepper's office. He's not available right now. How can I help you?"

I cringed. The poor woman. Likely bound by some internal protocol, she'd have to play along, all the while knowing her boss wasn't ever going to come back again. I'd met Harvey's assistant on a few occasions. She was a lovely witch who obviously adored her abrasive boss. There was no doubt she would mourn his passing for some time to come.

"Hello, Harriet. It's Holly Boldt."

"Oh, Holly." She sniffled. "Have you heard?"

"Yes. I'm so sorry."

"Me too."

"Harriet, I have to ask—this morning, when Harvey walked out of the council hearing, where did he go?"

Harriet sniffed again. "I—I'm really not sure, Holly. As far as I knew, he was planning to be busy all morning. I assumed it was because of your hearing but when your lawyer called, he told me Harvey left midway through."

"That's right. No idea where he went?"

"He called me, must have been close to nine o'clock, and told me he was done with the hearing and had been called away to a meeting. I thought it was strange because there wasn't anything on his schedule and even after he called, the ledger didn't update. Normally, it shifts and shuffles as he goes through his day so I always know where he's at. It's enchanted with a tracking spell but his signal wasn't anywhere. That only happens when he leaves the haven."

I nodded, trying to wedge the new fragments of information together. "Does he normally leave the haven?"

"He hates leaving the haven and he definitely wouldn't be in a taxi cab. You know—*knew*—Harvey. He liked the finer things in life. He would have used the portal to go into Seattle if he was going somewhere on foot. And if he needed a car, he would have used an SPA-owned town car. He never would have used a human taxi."

The sight *would* raise a few eyebrows. Harvey, with his pointed ears, sharp teeth, and spider-like hands, would have had trouble fitting in outside the haven. The only SPA agents who worked outside the haven system were ones who could seamlessly blend in with humans so as to not alert them to the existence of creatures that filled both their storybooks and nightmares.

"Harriet, I hate to ask, but what did Harvey have to say about my hearing? Were you under the impression he was prepared to testify on my behalf?"

"As far as I knew. He didn't say much about it but when he left this morning that was his first stop."

I sighed. I knew Harvey trusted Harriet implicitly but I didn't want to risk uncovering his secrets by telling her he'd promised to bury evidence to keep me out of trouble. It was likely best to keep that detail to myself, at least for the time being.

"He cared about you very much, dear. Harvey was a complicated soul. His mind worked in ways that most wouldn't understand. I know he was tough on you, but he had your best interests at heart. That much I know for certain. He must have had a very good reason for leaving the hearing without providing his testimony."

A bittersweet warmth spread through me, taking away some of the doubt that had lingered there since the moment I'd turned and found his place on the bench abandoned. "Thank you, Harriet." Tears welled up in the corners of my eyes. "I appreciate your time and I'm so sorry for your —*our*—loss."

"Thank you, Holly. You take care of yourself, okay?"

"I will." I ended the call and set the phone beside me on the bed.

Before I could reflect too much, somebody knocked on my door. I cinched the robe tight again and padded out to check the security peephole. Teddy stood there, looking worried. I released the security ward and opened the door. He hurried into the room and I set the ward once again.

"Hear from your friend at the Herald?" I asked him.

Teddy gave a quick nod. "It looks like Harvey might have been poisoned. The SPA agents on the scene found a cup of coffee laced with some kind of potion inside the taxi cab. My guy's source is within the SPA and he said they're taking it back to headquarters for further testing."

"Poisoned?" I gulped. It was a risky way to kill someone. Potions held a magical signature of the wizard or witch who'd crafted it. Granted, there were several ways around it, but it took skill and know-how. Most witches and wizards who weren't savvy in the world of potion crafting didn't even realize there was a way to trace the magic required to pull the ingredients together into a viable potion.

"The human who called it in said he was going back to work after a smoke break; he works at one of the factories in that part of town. He says it's rare to have cars, especially cabs, around. He walked up thinking something untoward might be going on and found Harvey with his face pressed up against the glass, mouth open." Teddy stopped and raised a hand. "I won't get into all of the details but it was quite a shock to the young man. He called the police but the SPA caught wind of the dispatch call, figured something super might be involved, and sent agents to the scene."

"How awful. Poor Harvey." I shuddered. "No one else saw anything?"

Teddy shook his head. "At least no one has come forward yet."

"I called Harvey's assistant," I said, then relayed what Harriet had told me over the phone.

"His voicemail said he was out on business, but that doesn't match up with what we've heard. Especially the mode of transportation and the fact that he was alone. If there was some kind of operation or emergency, he would have been with other agents. They would have taken cars or the portals into the city."

"It doesn't make sense. Why would someone want to kill Harvey?" I paced in front of the couch. "I should go and offer my assistance. Maybe I could help them trace the potion or see where the ingredients came from? I could—"

"Holly," Teddy interjected gently. "The SPA has it covered. They're not going to let someone outside the agency come in and step on the investigation. Besides that …" He paused and shifted his eyes around the room, as though only just realizing his surroundings.

"What?"

His gaze circled back to me. "Holly, there's something else ... another clue."

The low tone of his voice set my heart racing. "What is it, Teddy?"

He swallowed hard and wrung his hands together. "There was a note in Harvey's pocket. It said: *choose your allies carefully.*"

I blinked. "And you think that means *me?*"

"We don't know, Holly. But it does seem a little coincidental. He gets called away in the middle of your hearing, where he's agreed to testify on your behalf, and the next thing we know, he's found poisoned, with this threatening note. I feel it's better to be safe than sorry. I've canceled the request for a follow-up hearing before the council and I think it would be best if we both headed back to Beechwood Harbor. We need to let the SPA handle this case before we plan our next move."

My pulse continued to race long after Teddy went back to his room to make the travel arrangements.

CHAPTER 6

Adam arrived a couple of hours later, and from the sound in the hallway, Evangeline was with him. I hurried to open the door, with Boots weaving around my ankles. "Hey you guys," I said, pulling the door open wide. Boots marched out into the hall and swirled around Evangeline's legs. She bent and scooped him up into her arms and he immediately batted at the end of the long, raven braid that hung over one shoulder. I smiled and stepped back to usher them into the room.

Adam frowned at me. "You didn't ask me for the password," he said, rooting himself in the hallway.

"Password?" I repeated, glancing at Evangeline. She sighed.

"To make sure I'm who I say I am. I texted it to you on the drive here. Didn't you see it?"

"No, I didn't." I shook my head. "Tell you what—I'm going to do a visual confirmation." I stepped back and gave him a once-over. "You're all clear, St. James."

Evangeline giggled and swept into the room, Boots propped on her hip as though he were a chubby toddler instead of an overgrown tabby cat. "Ignore him. He's gone full-blown Jack Bauer since you called about the note they found. I had to listen to his insane ramblings all the way here." She waved a hand.

She surveyed the suite as she wandered further inside until her eyes snagged on the bottle of wine sitting on the wet bar. "Hello, lovely." She glanced at me, a Cheshire smile on her face. "Mind if I break into this?"

I laughed softly and waved a hand. "Help yourself." I turned back to Adam, whose frown was deeply etched into his handsome face. I sighed. "Fine, Adam. What's the password?"

"Pistachios."

I glanced over my shoulder at Evangeline and she rolled her eyes. I smiled at Adam. "Great. You got it on the first try. Now, please, come inside."

Adam growled, mumbling under his breath as he stalked into the room. "I don't know why I bother."

"None of us do, dear," Evangeline replied.

I suppressed a smile. "I didn't know you were coming too, Evangeline."

She's poured two *large* glasses of wine and handed one to me with a "you're gonna need it" look on her face. "Adam wanted to borrow my car and when he told me what happened, I decided to tag along. I'm so sorry, Holly. About the hearing and, of course, about Harvey."

"Thanks."

"Where's Teddy?" she asked before taking a sip of her wine.

"His room is right next door."

She set Boots down. He landed with a hefty thump and then wove around her legs. "I'm going to go say hello."

Evangeline swept from the room, leaving Adam and me alone with the palpable tension of his frustration. I sighed deeply when the door closed. "I'm sorry about the password thing, Adam."

He stepped closer and pulled me into his arms. "I only want to keep you safe. If someone targeted Harvey because he was helping you, that means you have some powerful enemies."

"We don't know that's what happened." I relaxed against his chest and smiled slightly as the smell of pine and cedar swirled around me like a comforting blanket. Adam always smelled like the forest—like trees and fresh, clear river water, all bathed in sunshine.

I couldn't fault him for being overprotective at times. It was quite literally in his nature. Not only was Adam a shifter—which, on its own guaranteed a protective streak—but as a large predatory animal, he was even more bent toward being territorial and fierce. For the most part I didn't mind. Stars, sometimes I downright enjoyed it. I had a tendency to get myself in over my head and found it comforting to know Adam would always have my back. I'd learned to take the good with the occasionally annoying.

Adam dropped a quick kiss to my lips. "You taste like wine," he said, his eyes gleaming.

I kissed him again and then pulled out of reach before things got too heated. As appealing as the idea was, it didn't quite feel right given the events of the day.

"How are you doing?" he asked.

"Shaken, I guess? I don't really know what to think. I want to get out there and do something. To help in some way."

Adam nodded. "I know you do, but it's safer if we stay here until the morning. Then we'll head back to Beechwood Harbor."

"I shouldn't have even tried. The hearing was a complete waste of time and now ... this."

"You had to try, gorgeous." He cocked his head. "Wait until this is resolved and then you and Teddy can talk about the next steps. There must be something he can do."

I shrugged. "I don't know about that. You should have seen them, Adam. They were so smug and spiteful. None of them really seemed like they wanted to be there and that one witch ... whatever her name is ... she acted like I'd personally offended her or something."

"And you're sure you've never met her before? You said she was younger than the rest of the council members. Is it possible you went to academy together? Or maybe rival academies?"

"Not that I can think of. I've been racking my brain trying to figure it out. None of it makes any sense. The sham of a hearing, Harvey leaving before testifying, and now his death." I shook my head. "Teddy says he was poisoned."

"Really?"

"Hopefully they'll get a lock on the signature."

Adam raised an eyebrow. "Signature?"

"Potions carry the signature of the maker. The magic that's used to create the potion leaves behind a trace. Every potion maker has their own unique identifier."

Adam blinked, surprised by the kernel of information. "So this should be pretty open and shut then, right? I mean, if all they have to do is discern some markings."

"Not necessarily," I countered, beginning to pace the room. "First of all, unless the murderer is a potion maker, it's unlikely the signature will lead directly to them. Most likely, they purchased the potion. Obviously, the kinds of potions that can kill aren't sold in the corner shops or from private potion masters. So, either the potion was sold on the black magic market or the killer has an innate knowledge of potion work and was able to blend two or more innocuous formulas together to create a deadly concoction."

"What happens to the signatures then?"

"They become muddled. Hard, if not impossible, to read. The other problem is that even if the potions are tracked back to the master who made them, it still doesn't tell the SPA who mixed them and dosed Harvey. Regulated potion shops and masters have to keep detailed record of what's being sold. But those who sell on the black magic market aren't as ... *stringent* with their bookkeeping."

A crooked grin tugged at the corners of Adam's mouth. "So, before Harvey shut you down, you were selling your potions on this black magic market?"

"Well—I uh—it was a little different." My cheeks warmed. "I wasn't selling anything dangerous or forbidden!"

Adam tugged me back into his arms. "I always knew you were trouble, Holly Boldt."

"Yeah, yeah, yeah." I rolled my eyes and pulled away, then waved a hand at the sleek cabinet Evangeline had already raided. "If you're hungry, there're some snacks in the mini bar."

"How'd you know?" he asked, grinning.

"Well, besides the fact that your stomach is a black hole, you decided the safety password should be *pistachios*. I took an educated guess."

Adam chuckled and went to rummage through the mini bar. He carried the loot over to the couch and popped the top on a can of peanuts. He took a handful and started munching even as his expression darkened. "Not to be insensitive, but without Harvey, what are the chances of a second hearing going through?"

"Not good."

"I'm sorry, gorgeous."

I flopped onto the couch beside him and sighed. "Me too."

"I'm sure Cassie would jump at the chance to have you back at Siren's Song full time."

"It's not so much the money that's the problem," I replied softly. "I've managed to save most of the reward money I earned with Nick after that fiasco with Georgia Banks."

"Holly, you won't work at a coffee shop for the rest of your life. You'll figure something else out."

His words were meant to be comforting but they only added to the twisting anxiety in my stomach. All my life, I'd stood out from other witches and wizards. I showed exceptional talent for potion work when I was very young, and my mother, and then my Aunt Bethany, had fostered it.

I was the one the family put their faith in. They believed I was destined to go on and do amazing things, to rise up past the stigma of the Boldt family name and prove that Boldt witches were more than trouble makers and outcasts. So far, I'd managed to be arrested three times, and trailed by the SPA for the majority of my adult life for a crime I didn't commit. Just when I was finally breaking free of all those obstacles, the hope of starting a new life was squashed right before my eyes. How was I supposed to bounce back from that kind of crushing blow?

Adam's chocolate eyes stared down at me, etched with concern. He brushed a strand of my hair away from my face and tucked it gently behind my ear. "Gorgeous, I hate seeing you like this. What can I do to help? Want me to go out and get you some Lemon Clouds?" he asked with a smile.

"No, thank you." I laughed and burrowed into his side. "I've already had way more than I'm willing to admit to over the last twenty-four hours."

Adam chuckled. "Sounds serious if you're not even willing to tell *me* how many you've had. I'm not exactly the snack police. If anything, I've corrupted you. Turned you full-blown grazer."

"Once we get back to Beechwood Harbor we might need to check into some kind of twelve-step program."

We sat together in silence, wading through our own thoughts, until someone knocked softly on the door. Adam untangled his arm from around me and went to answer it. A smile pulled at my lips as he tried to open it, only to realize it was warded shut. "A little help here, gorgeous," he said.

I waved my hand and a pulse of magic zeroed in and released the ward. Adam stumbled back as the door flew open. Evangeline and Teddy came into the room and my eyebrows hiked up as I noted their hands were clasped together. Evangeline was the one who'd introduced me to Teddy in the first place, and while I'd had my suspicions that they were more than *just* friends, I hadn't seen any concrete proof.

Adam locked the door but didn't ask me to reset the ward. He came back to join me on the couch. Teddy waved his hand and let Evangeline take the armchair. She sat and he stood behind her, his hands planted on the back of the sleek chair.

"How are you feeling, Holly?" Evangeline asked.

"Honestly? I think I've gone numb."

Teddy gave an understanding nod. "I spoke with my friend from the Haven Herald. According to his source, the scene has been cleared and they're officially calling it a murder. The other details will come in over the next few days, I'm sure. Knowing the SPA, they'll probably try to keep this out of the papers as long as possible, but I would expect it to be public knowledge within the next twenty-four hours. If you'd like, I can stay in Beechwood Harbor and take on the press on your behalf."

"The press?" My brows wrinkled. "Why would the press be interested in me?"

"The council records will go public. Those records will show that Harvey was at your hearing prior to his death. I'd be shocked if the media doesn't come sniffing around for information."

I sighed. "Great."

"The SPA also wants to speak with both of us. I've arranged the interviews for first thing in the morning. After that, we can all head back to Beechwood Harbor."

Evangeline moved to the edge of her seat and offered a kind smile. "Teddy will handle everything, Holly. You don't have to worry."

I nodded, but her comforting words only went so far. Despite my track record, I actually preferred *not* to be the one in the center of these situations. Yet, despite my best efforts, I continued to get tangled up in situations that quickly swallowed me up until I was in way over my head.

Something told me things were going to get a lot worse before they got better.

CHAPTER 7

Despite Teddy's assurances, a sharp knock on the door interrupted our room-service dinner a few hours later. Adam answered it and begrudgingly ushered two SPA agents into the room. According to their badges, both of the agents were shifters. The first was a tall, broad-shouldered woman named Aggy Bramble, an eagle-shifter. Her face was all sharp angles except for her nose, which looked as though it had been broken on more than one occasion and hadn't set properly, giving it a crooked appearance that threw off the straight lines of the rest of her features. Her partner, Vincent Mache, was a bear-shifter and looked the part. He towered a few inches above his statuesque partner and was twice as broad, with burly muscles that bulged under the skin-tight black t-shirt he wore.

Teddy greeted the agents with a curt nod. "I was told we would be interviewed in the morning."

Agent Mache crossed his arms. "We don't have time to waste on a case like this. Not when the victim is one of our own," he said, his gaze cold. It was almost like he was waiting for Teddy to argue. What would he do then? Slam him against the wall? It looked as though he could level Teddy flat with a simple tap to the chest.

"It's fine," I hurried to interject. I stood and brushed my fingers off on a napkin before extending a hand toward the female agent. "I'm Holly Boldt."

Evangeline took my lead and jumped up as well. She busied herself at the mini bar, preparing each of the agents a tall glass of spritzer water with lime and lemon wedges. At one point, her eagerness to please would have driven me batty, but I'd known her long enough to know it was just her nature. Ever the hostess.

"Thank you for agreeing to meet with us, Ms. Boldt," Agent Bramble began. "I do apologize if there was a mix-up in the timing. But as my partner has already stated, this investigation is going to be running around the clock until we get some answers. Harvey would have demanded nothing less."

I smiled down at my hands. "That's probably true."

"Harvey was a dear friend," she continued. "He will be greatly missed both inside the agency as well as personally."

I gave a solemn nod, hit by an unexpected wave of emotion in light of the agent's words.

"As far as we know, Ms. Boldt and Mr. Trevail, you were two of the last people to have seen Harvey alive, so we'd like to ask a few questions. We're trying to establish a firm timeline of the day's events leading up to the attack," Agent Mache explained. "Harvey's assistant, Harriet, told us he arrived at his office a little after eight o'clock this morning. He checked in with his support staff and then departed to meet you at Council Hall, where he was to provide testimony."

"That's correct," Teddy answered evenly.

"What time did he arrive?"

"Promptly at nine o'clock," Teddy said.

Agent Mache looked to me for confirmation and I nodded.

"All right," he continued. "What time did the hearing conclude?"

"Mr. Colepepper didn't stay for the duration of the hearing," Teddy said. "I don't know exactly when he left, but it couldn't have been more than ten minutes into the proceedings. I can furnish the detailed minutes of the hearing. They're brief," he added his voice tinged with irritation.

Evangeline swept in and served the drinks, breaking the tension with a sweet smile. Each of the agents thanked her. She took a seat beside Teddy and rested her hand on his knee, the picture of elegance and composure. I nearly smiled despite the seriousness of the moment. She was truly a master.

Agent Bramble picked up the questions as her partner paused to take a drink. His hand, nearly the size of a catcher's mitt, dwarfed the crystal glass.

"So," she asked, "when Harvey left the hearing, he didn't say *anything*?"

I shook my head. "One minute he was there, the next he was gone."

Teddy cleared his throat, silently reminding me that he was the one answering the questions. "Mr. Colepepper was set to testify and vanished before he was able to. The council called for a break and I attempted to call Mr. Colepepper several times but was unable to reach him."

Agent Bramble frowned at Agent Mache who didn't look her way. "How did he appear? At the hearing," Agent Mache asked.

"He seemed normal to me." I shrugged one shoulder. I'd played the memory of the morning over and over again in my mind but couldn't pick out anything specific that might be helpful. "He mentioned being swamped. Caught up with the Praxle case."

"Who isn't," Mache grumbled under his breath.

Agent Bramble gave him an annoyed look before asking, "Ms. Boldt, I hate to ask, but you've known Harvey for over half your life."

I didn't need to be reminded. Harvey had first entered my life following the murder of my parents. His role in my life was two-fold: to protect me and to keep me from causing trouble. After everything with Gabriel and his ring of dark and dangerous friends, I was thrust under even closer examination and saw Harvey on a bi-monthly basis. The meetings mostly served as a reminder that the SPA was watching me. Closely.

Agent Bramble continued, "Can you think of anyone who would want to harm him?"

I shook my head. "Harvey was—well, he was an *acquired* taste. I'd be lying if I said we'd always had a smooth relationship. He was about as straight-forward as they come and sure, sometimes that might have ruffled feathers." I cringed, wondering if the expression was offensive to an eagle-shifter. Agent Bramble didn't appear to notice the questionable turn of phrase. "If it were me, I'd start with his recent case files and see who might have been on his radar."

She bristled, her thin lips twisting into a scowl. "Thank you, Ms. Boldt," she replied, her tone icy.

"I'm sorry." I sighed. "Obviously that's what you intend to do. I wasn't thinking."

Agent Mache frowned, then finished the rest of his drink.

I dropped my eyes to the coffee table between us.

"Do you have any questions for us?" Agent Mache asked me.

I glanced up. "Will I be assigned a new agent?"

The hulking bear-shifter turned to his partner and

offered a wry expression. "Agent Bramble will be filling in as your liaison to the SPA until a proper case worker can be established."

I met the sharp eyes of Agent Bramble and my stomach flip-flopped. "Wonderful."

THE FOLLOWING MORNING, we all piled into Evangeline's tiny sports car and set off back to Beechwood Harbor. The trip normally took a little over three hours, but Evangeline had relinquished the keys to Adam and he was driving the car like he'd stolen it, completely ignoring the daggers Teddy was throwing from his place in the cramped back seat. I caught him glaring at the back of Adam's head in the rearview mirror and had to suppress a laugh. The two of them were polar opposites in every regard. Adam was the poster child for rebellion—leather jackets, rakish smile, and devil-my-care attitude. Teddy likely slept in a three-piece suit and probably didn't have so much as a speeding ticket on his record.

"You do realize this is a *forty-five* zone?" Teddy finally chimed in.

Adam laughed but he took his foot off the gas and let the car coast for a few minutes as we wrapped around the curving roads that led away from the city and back to the Washington coast. We weren't close enough that I could smell the sea in the air, but the lush trees that lined both sides of the two-lane highway started to sooth my nerves. I was on my way home. Every mile that flew by was one more between me and the mess back inside the haven. Beyond that, I simply missed my routine. Shopping at Thistle, the small natural food market, and seeing familiar faces each morning at the coffee shop. I loved being able to identify every face walking the downtown streets after dinner. There was something reassuring about living in a close-knit community. An unexpected freedom found in the sense of familiarity.

Boots sat on my lap, calmly watching the scenery whiz by as we turned onto another curvy road. I smiled down at him as my fingers worked through his thick, tawny fur. "You don't mind the speed, do you, Bootsie?"

Teddy muttered something behind me and I had no doubt his scowl had shifted from the back of Adam's head to my own.

"It'll be fine, Teddy," Evangeline said soothingly. "This car has so many safety charms that it would quite literally take a meteor shower to do any damage."

"Really?" I asked, twisting around to look at her.

She nodded. "Originally it was charmed by my security team when I was working on *The Wednesday Witch*. If you think human paparazzi are terrible, you can only *imagine* how awful they can be when they're bestowed with magic." She grimaced. "I hired a security team to follow me around at all times to make sure I was safe. They called themselves the King's Guard. Although, as far as I know, they never actually guarded royalty. Seems like I found that out after I signed the contracts. In any case, they proved to be quite good at their jobs so I forgave them the slightly dubious branding."

"Impressive," Adam said. "I've heard about them before. They're kind of legends."

Evangeline nodded. "Quinton, he's a wizard, though some say he leans more into sorcery. I didn't really care, as long as he could provide the charms I needed. Anyway, he's the one who charmed this car to be pretty close to indestructible."

"Still," Teddy interjected. "I'd rather not put it to the test."

Adam gave a disappointed frown.

The rest of the trip was mostly spent talking about trivial things. It was obvious we were all attempting to tip-toe around the murder or anything relating to my failed council hearing. In the end, Adam flipped on the radio and we all fell into a comfortable silence.

We pulled up in front of the Beechwood Manor a little after noon. Boots jumped out the open window as soon as the car came to a stop and made a beeline around the house, his bottle-brush tail straight as an arrow, likely headed for the back door, which was equipped with a doggy door straight into the kitchen.

"Apparently someone missed home," Adam said, watching from the driver's seat.

"More like he wonders if he missed out on something in his food bowl."

Adam scoffed. "Well if the undead princess is even awake, I doubt she's going to show him much compassion."

I didn't argue. Lacey and Boots weren't exactly BFFs.

We all laughed and then got out of the car and gathered the bags from the trunk. Posy was waiting in the entryway to greet us. Her silver-purple silhouette shimmered with excitement as I followed Adam inside. "Holly, dear! How did your hearing go?"

Apparently no one had told her what happened.

Evangeline cringed as she joined me. "I'm sorry, Posy. Teddy and I tried to find you last night before we left."

Posy's smile fell away. "I was with Gwen. She dragged me to a ghost support group."

We all stared, dumbfounded by the revelation. Half a dozen follow-up questions popped into my mind.

"Um, did you say you were at a ghost *support* group?" Adam ventured.

Posy scoffed and flapped a translucent hand through the

air. "She's been on me for months, ever since Katerina was here. I mostly went along to get her off my back."

I shoved aside my questions and filed them away under the mental label of "entertaining conversations for another time."

"Well, to be honest, Posy, the hearing didn't go so well."

"Oh no. I'm so sorry, dear. I hoped having Mr. Colepepper's testimony would make it a sure thing."

All of us glanced around the room, choosing different focal points.

"What?" Posy asked.

"Harvey was called away before he could testify to anything." I drew in a deep breath. "And then … well, he was found murdered last night."

Posy's bespectacled eyes went wide. Her mouth worked as she struggled to find the right words and eventually sputtered, "Murdered? Holly, I'm so—that's simply—how horrifying! Do they know what happened?"

I shook my head. "It's all still under investigation. We met with the SPA agents in charge of the case last night at the hotel."

"Well I'm very sorry to hear that, dear. He was a lovely man … troll … creature."

A pounding sounded from down the hall off to the right of the grand staircase.

"Um, what was that?" I asked Posy.

"That's not …," Evangeline started, shifting a cautious eye to Adam.

Adam shut the front door. "I *knew* we were forgetting something."

CHAPTER 8

"Should I even ask?" I said with my eyes squeezed closed. I had a feeling I knew who was doing the pounding but was silently praying I was wrong.

I peeled one eye open and swiveled it in Adam's direction. He gave Evangeline a sheepish glance. I opened both eyes and stared at Evangeline. She shifted her weight from one leg to the other and refused to look at me.

"That's Nick," Adam finally admitted.

I cringed. "You left Nick alone in the manor all night? With Lacey?"

"We got your call and just kinda ... left," Adam explained. "He was still sleeping off the massive dose of sleeping potion Evie fed him!"

I waved my hand toward the frantic pounding sound. "Well clearly that is no longer the case!"

"I sealed the door from the outside," Evangeline chimed in. "He can't get out and Lacey can't get in."

I threw my hands up in the air. "How am I supposed to explain that to him? Oops, sorry Nick, I didn't realize my roomies would drug you and then barricade you in a dark room for twenty-four hours. Please don't be mad."

"That's not helping, Holly." Adam ground his teeth together. "What are we going to do? Are you sure you can't wipe his memory?"

"For the millionth time, *no!*" I rubbed my temples. "I don't do mind magic. It's too risky. Especially when he's already been ... treated. I meant to ask—well, I was planning to ask Harvey about the options. He's the only one I trust."

I raked my fingers through my hair. *Think, think, think.*

"I could give him more tea," Evangeline offered quietly. "Buy us some more time."

"No!" I boomed, my voice much louder than I'd intended.

The four faces staring at me all flinched at once. Evangeline's face crumpled and Teddy wrapped an arm around her shoulders and led her off toward the kitchen. Guilt slid down deep into my gut. I'd have to mend those fences later.

"Hello? Can anyone hear me! Help!" Nick's frantic cries came down the hall.

"Ugh! This is ridiculous." I stormed down the hallway, scraping my mind for what kind of tale I could spin to make the circumstances any less bizarre.

I came up empty.

With a flick of my hand, I released the lock Evangeline had set and pulled the door open. Nick, his dark hair sticking out in every possible direction, blinked a few times. "Holly?"

I drew in a quick breath and slapped a smile on my face. "Hello, Nick."

Nick squinted at me. "What are you—what's going on? What time—what *day* is it?"

"It's Tuesday. A little after noon, I think. Are you feeling better? Adam and Evangeline told me you stopped by late last night and fell asleep on the couch. Let me guess, they made you watch that movie with the talking dog? I know, it's the worst. I fall asleep every time too."

Adam stood at my side. "Sorry man, I thought you'd dig it."

It was the most absurd lie, but I had no idea what else to say. I needed some kind of plausible—if not logical—reason for his overnight stay in the manor's formal study.

"I—uh—" He exhaled. "I guess so? Is there even a TV in here?" he asked, craning back to look inside the study.

"Come on," I said, gesturing for him to follow me. "Let's get you some lunch."

He stayed rooted in place. "Why was the door locked?"

"Oh, that,"—I flapped a hand and smiled—"Boots recently figured out how to open doorknobs. He's so tall! He gets up there and works his little paws—," I mimed a strange series of gestures.

Adam snorted.

I shot him a glare. *Not helping*.

When I looked back at Nick, he was frowning. "The *cat* opens doors?"

"Uh-huh." I rocked back on my heels. "How do you feel about nachos for lunch? I know I sure could go for some right about now."

Nick stared at Adam and me for another long moment but finally gave a tentative nod. "Yeah, okay."

Adam led the way back down the hall, past the stairs, and into the kitchen. I breathed a sigh of relief when I saw that Evangeline and Teddy were already at work making some coffee. "Look who's up!" I told them, my voice artificially bright and sunny.

Evangeline's eyes went wide with recognition. "Oh good!"

"I told you guys not to make people watch that terrible movie," I prompted to Evangeline. "Put poor Nick right to sleep."

Her eyebrows lifted and I cringed, mouthing *I know*. I mimed smacking myself on the forehead while Nick's back was turned.

"That's all right," Nick finally said. "I've had a cold the last few days and I think it's making my head fuzzy. I probably took too much nighttime syrup. Thanks for letting me sleep it off here."

"Not a problem," Evangeline said, obviously relieved he'd swallowed the painfully thin cover story.

"Adam and Evangeline told me you were out of town," Nick said, turning back to me.

"I just got home. The trip was shorter than expected."

Adam went to work pulling out the ingredients for his massive, six-layer nacho platter—one of his custom creations—and I brought over sugar and cream for the coffee. Evangeline and Nick sat down at the table after we assured them there was nothing they could do to help. The manor kitchen was large, but not quite big enough for five adults—and one begging tabby cat—to work comfortably side by side.

I dropped the sugar and cream off at the table and then hauled Boots into my arms and deposited him on his cat bed. "Stay there and I'll give you a treat," I told him with a waggle of my finger. "We don't need you tripping someone."

He frowned up at me but then remembered the promise of the treat and sat down, his haunches sticking out from his rotund backside.

"Good boy."

I took a seat at the table, on the other side of Nick. Teddy brought over the coffee and then went back to grab some mugs. Within a few minutes, everyone except Adam had a cup of hot coffee and was seated at the table.

"You sure you don't need any help?" Evangeline asked Adam.

He craned his head around with a grin. "Let the master work."

I rolled my eyes. "Trust me, Evangeline—it's better if you don't know the secrets to his nachos. They're delicious but there are probably some questionable ingredients."

"Hey!" Adam said, shooting me a playful scowl.

I held up my hands. "I'm just saying, you're a snack-food genius, but you also call marshmallow fluff *food*."

"Well rest assured, there isn't a speck of fluff on these bad boys."

"I'd hope not," Teddy said indignantly. He turned in his seat and eyed the stack of take-out menus piled on one end of the counter. He was clearly making back-up lunch plans.

"This is nice!" Posy said, floating through the closed kitchen door. "I do love having a full house for a meal. It reminds me of when Earl and I used to host out of town family and friends for the holidays."

I looked over my shoulder at Posy. "That's sweet."

"Who are you talking to?" Nick asked.

Bat wings!

I whipped around and plastered on a faux smile. "Boots."

Never mind that he was in the opposite corner of the kitchen.

"Oh dear," Posy said, suddenly at my side. I forced myself to not watch her as she considered Nick. "I forgot he was still here. I think he saw me last night, out in the garden."

Teddy, Evangeline, and I all shifted our eyes toward her. He'd seen Posy? How was that even possible? And if so, why couldn't he see her now? Was there some kind of rule that ghosts could only be seen at night? My heart pounded harder. Nick glanced up and frowned at the strained expressions on our faces. "You guys okay?"

Adam swooped in with a cookie sheet of nachos. "Voila!"

"That was fast," Teddy said, his skepticism ratcheting up another notch.

Adam grinned. "The magic of a microwave."

Posy scoffed. "That beastly thing!"

"I think they look great!" I chimed in, reaching for a chip.

Everyone followed my lead and dug in with extra exuberance—even Teddy—and shifted the conversation to something completely benign: Sports. Adam, Teddy, and Nick launched into an intense debate about the upcoming March Madness ... whatever *that* was. Evangeline and I rolled our eyes at each other and Posy floated off through the ceiling. I made a mental note to track her down after Nick left to ask exactly what had prompted her to think he'd seen her the night before.

After the last chip had been devoured, Nick announced he needed to get home and shower and try to put in a few hours at the office. He'd been behind schedule thanks to the cold—and I imagined more than a few sleepless nights—and needed to try to get something productive done for the day. I walked him to the door and said goodbye, then watched him until he was nearly out of sight before closing the door.

I sagged against it and exhaled a deep breath. Was my life ever going to go back to being blissfully boring?

∼

LATER THAT AFTERNOON, after a much-needed nap, I left the manor. I didn't have a solid plan in place, so I decided to go for a walk to clear my mind. I circled my way around town, wandering through the quiet residential pockets, before going downtown. As I walked, the tangled ball of thoughts inside my mind started to unwind a bit.

After lunch, Teddy had gone to the study to make some phone calls and try to figure out a plan for my next move. I'd get a full report when I got back to the manor, but for the moment all I had to go by were the events that had transpired over the past forty-eight hours. It was hard to imagine a scenario where a second council hearing would go any differently. Teddy assured me there was a chance, but that was in his nature as a superstar lawyer. Part of me wondered if I shouldn't call the whole thing off and avoid another humiliating—not to mention pointless—council hearing. I wasn't sure I'd be able to reign in my anger if the second hearing had the same result as the first. As it was, I'd barely avoided landing back in a jail cell.

What would my future look like without potion making? I could still tend to my garden beds and the myriad of plants in my greenhouse. Assuming the banishment wasn't made permanent, I could travel to and from the havens so I could no doubt make quite a nice income selling top-quality plant material and potion ingredients to the shops. I could become a top supplier and become renowned for having prize-winning plants.

Would that be enough? I loved the time spent in my garden but had always considered it a necessary part of being a potions witch living outside the haven; it wasn't something I'd set out to do commercially. Not to mention the manor's backyard wasn't equipped to handle the scope of gardening I'd need to do in order to keep up with demand if I were to attempt it full time. In addition, I'd have to buy a car or truck to cart the supplies to and from the haven.

Then there was Adam. He'd made it clear he had no intention of ever living in the haven system again. While I was currently disenchanted enough to agree with him, I wasn't sure it was a lifelong commitment. Being three hours away wasn't so bad, and I had missed Beechwood Harbor during my time in the city, but if I wanted a future outside of potion making, I'd have far better opportunities inside the haven. Wouldn't I? Or would it be like before—taking menial jobs there because people were leery of my reputation?

If I stayed in Beechwood Harbor, I would be fine. Everyone liked me well enough and I had a job, friends, and a makeshift family. The type of support system that ensured I wouldn't spend birthdays or the holidays alone. I was happy. Wasn't I?

It all circled back to one thing: potions.

It was the missing piece and I couldn't seem to find a way to rearrange the other pieces of my life to make up for that void.

With that miserably drawn conclusion, I trudged back to the manor. On the way, I passed Evangeline as she wandered down the opposite side of the street, likely on her way to The Emerald. She waved me over. "Close call this morning!" she said with a grin. I followed her around the corner and we stopped at the front door of her spa. "I'm sorry we forgot Nick was at the house, Holly. I hope you're not too mad at us. I don't think any damage was done."

"I'm not mad," I assured her.

She pushed into the day spa and Lucy, who was sitting at the reception desk, greeted us. She clicked through something on the thin computer monitor and then filled Evangeline in on the events of the morning, then offered to give me a manicure since her first client of the day had canceled.

I shrugged and took my place at her work station. I wasn't one to turn down a fresh manicure. Lucy joined me and started soaking my fingers to get rid of the polish she'd put on a week ago. With no customers in the spa, Evangeline and I told Lucy about the events of the last few days. She was a telepath but had grown up in the human world, not understanding her abilities. She hadn't learned anything about the supernatural world until a few years back. Needless to say, she found the entire story overwhelming.

As she was finishing up the top coat of clear polish, Ben, the masseur and resident town beefcake, came out from behind the thick emerald curtain that separated the back of the spa from the retail space.

"Hey, Holly," he called out, his arms laden with boxes. "I'm glad you're back in town! I could really use another batch of that salve you made for my hands when you get a chance."

With her back to him, Evangeline cringed and mouthed *sorry*.

"I'll see what I can do," I told him with a polite smile.

"Great, thanks!" He crossed the shop and backed up against the front door to let himself out. "I'm off. See you tomorrow."

Evangeline wriggled her fingers. "Have a nice night."

Lucy and I waved and echoed her sentiment.

Ben pushed out the door and Evangeline frowned over at me. "Sorry about that," she said. "He was asking where you'd gone and I said you went into the haven to get some supplies and would be back in business when you got back. I didn't think there was any way your petition could possibly get denied."

I scoffed. "Yeah. Me either."

"I'm so sorry, Holly. If you need a job, I can hire you to help out around here. Half-price discount on product, excellent benefits, and the free perk of getting to ogle Ben all day long. Although Adam might not appreciate that last part."

I laughed. "Yeah, probably not."

Evangeline nudged me with her hip as she passed by. "Not that he has to worry."

"What about you and Teddy? You two seemed pretty cozy."

Lucy gawked up at Evangeline. "You've been holding out on me!"

Evangeline laughed and waved a hand. "I keep telling you, we're just friends."

I raised a skeptical brow and arched it at Lucy, my meaning clear: *Yeah, right.*

Lucy giggled. "Well, here's a tip from your old married friend: make sure you get along with his mother before you start picking out wedding dresses and flower arrangements!"

We all laughed. Evangeline ducked her chin and considered her own manicured nails. "I shouldn't laugh ... Teddy's mother actually passed away several years ago."

Lucy held up a finger with a wicked grin. "Sold!"

I tried to stifle my laugh, but failed miserably. "Now, I'm not saying I want Adam's mother to die, but I certainly wouldn't be heartbroken if she suddenly relocated to somewhere far, far away."

"Like Australia?"

I grinned. "I was thinking more like the moon."

Lucy's eyes glittered. "Excellent! She can take Gordy's mother with her. I mean, hey, someone has to start colonizing it, right?"

CHAPTER 9

With my mood lightened and my nails polished to sleek perfection, I headed home, where a solemn Teddy was waiting to speak with me. Dark clouds rolled over my newly uplifted outlook as I followed him into the kitchen where he'd set up his temporary office.

"Should I be sitting down for this?" I asked after putting on the kettle to make some tea.

Teddy, who was sitting at the head of the table, shook his head. "It's nothing like that."

"Whew!"

He smiled politely. "I spoke with a representative at Council Hall today. They were able to access the final judgment from the hearing. It appears the council has decided not to enforce the banishment. You're officially free to come and go from any haven."

"That's good news," I said, although I wasn't sure how much I would be using that *privilege*.

"Yes. It bodes well for the petitions I've filed. I'm hoping to get before the council by the end of the month. First, I'll have to argue that the original hearing was biased, which means I need to figure out *why* it was biased."

"We need to figure out who that witch was—the young one."

Teddy nodded. "I asked the clerk today but they weren't able to disclose that information over the phone. Some asinine rule. Unfortunately, the council members tend to live very private lives and rarely allow their names to be released in the press for fear of revenge from unhappy petitioners."

"Gee, I wonder why. It's not like they're unfair and callous."

Teddy frowned at me.

Clearly I was not helping.

"In any case, once we clear that hurdle, we will be able to get before a new council and present our case. However, as you and I both know, without Harvey, it's going to be difficult to convince them. I've put in a request with his assistant to see if she can find any notations on what he planned to testify about. If we could find some kind of statement of intent, it might work just as well as his actual testimony."

"What do you need me to do?"

"Mostly, be patient with me. This process could take some finagling. The other thing I wanted to ask was whether or not you could think of anyone who would want to block you from becoming a potions master. The way that witch came out firing made it seem like more than just a decision based on your past. It seemed personal in nature."

"I agree," I sighed. "But I don't know why anyone would care. It's not like I was applying to be a potions master for the council or some other prestigious job. I just want to make my potions and sell them to supers who need them. That's all."

"I know that, but I wonder if maybe someone else might have a different perception of your intentions."

I shrugged. "If so, I have no idea. I'll go through a list of my clients and see if anything pops. Other than the people I sell to, the only other supers who would know about my ability are the ones who tested me in the academy, but that was so long ago, I can't imagine any of them caring."

"All right, well let me know what you come up with, if anything."

"I will." The kettle was boiling and I moved to fill a mug with a hefty scoop of tea leaves. It hadn't been raining on my walk home, but it was far from balmy outside and the chill of the brisk walk still clung to me. After everything that had happened, I decided a hot cup of tea and a long, leisurely soak in the tub was exactly what I needed to put the awful events behind me.

~

A FEW DAYS passed with no word from the Haven Council in reply to Teddy's petition, or from the SPA regarding Harvey's murder investigation. As Teddy predicted, the Haven Herald and *The Witch Wire* both picked up the story and were reporting on it around the clock. Unfortunately, it had reached a sticking point where the same tidbits were recycled every hour or so with nothing new added. Reporters had called trying to get a comment from me, as I was publicly known as one of the last people to see Harvey alive. Teddy fielded the calls and requests in between trying to figure out the identity and motive of the witch who had so vehemently opposed me at the hearing. He was also waiting to hear back from Harriet, Harvey's assistant, to see if she found a note or other documentation to provide to the council in lieu of his testimony.

Evangeline was kept busy at the spa as always and Adam was swamped with his own work, leaving me lonely and bored. My hours at Siren's Song had been dramatically cut back while I pursued my potions business, so I was left with large gaps in my day while everyone else was busy.

Boots and I puttered around in the greenhouse a few hours each day and I experimented with baking, thinking it might prove to be a suitable replacement for potion work. In the end, all it did was add a few thousand calories to my daily intake. One night after Siren's Song closed, I met Cassie for happy hour at McNally's. We chatted about life and our respective relationships. It was a nice break from the monotony of wandering aimlessly through the manor all day.

By the fourth day, I was full-blown stir-crazy and called Agent Bramble. She was my only real connection to what was going on with the investigation. Surprisingly, as soon as I called, she informed me I was on her list of people to call that day. She invited me to come to her office for a meeting that afternoon. I couldn't get her to discuss anything over the phone, but accepted the invitation and hurried to get ready.

After a quick shower and change of clothes, I went into the kitchen to find Adam sitting at the table, a jar of marshmallow fluff in one hand and a giant spoon in the other. He looked up as I pushed into the room and noted my outfit. "Where are you going?"

"I have a meeting with my new gal pal, Agent Bramble."

Adam pulled a face. "That should be fun. She seemed like a real party."

"Tell me about it. Does the SPA only hire supers who were born without a shred of personality, or do they just strip it away during their training process?"

Adam grinned as he waved his spoon through the air. "I don't know and I have no intention of finding out."

I laughed. "Probably for the best," I said, pointing at his

spoon. "I'm pretty sure SPA agents aren't allowed to eat garbage like that."

Adam grabbed the warehouse-store-sized jar of the revolting goo—that could easily double as Spackle or tile grout—and dug a huge dollop out. "What does she want to talk about?"

"I don't know yet. I'm assuming it's about Harvey, but for all I know, she might want to introduce me to my new case worker or grill me to make sure I'm respecting the council's orders and not secretly cooking up potions."

Adam arched a brow. "Not that you would ever do that."

"Yeah, yeah. I know. Trust me—I've learned my lesson." I paced across the kitchen and pulled open the fridge. Even though I'd be using the SPA portal and wouldn't have to drive to and from Seattle, I still wanted a little snack before leaving. It would lower the odds of me blowing half a week's worth of tip money on Lemon Clouds. "I'm pretty sure if I step one toe out of line, Agent Bramble will shift into an eagle and carry me off to her nest."

Adam chuckled. "Now there's a visual."

I frowned and pulled out a container of blueberries. They were out of season and cost a small fortune to buy fresh from Thistle, but it was my one vice. Okay, not counting Lemon Clouds and bear claws. Those particular treats had surpassed vice territory some time ago and had slid into the land of full-blown addiction.

"Any progress toward getting a second council hearing?" Adam asked when I joined him at the table.

"I don't know. With everything else going on, I haven't really given it much thought. Unless Teddy can get me a different panel, I doubt it would do much good."

"Still no clue who the witchy-witch was?"

I shook my head and popped a few blueberries in my

mouth. "He's trying to get a name. For whatever reason, it's like top-secret information."

"You want me to do a little digging?" Adam asked nonchalantly, as if being a super-spy was one of his side hobbies.

I arched a brow. "How are you planning on digging? The haven doesn't use technology. It's not like you can hack into their system or something."

"Oh ye of little faith." He smiled and polished off the last bit of the marshmallow fluff and returned the lid to the glass jar. "You're forgetting that my dad works for haven law enforcement. He didn't get to the top of his field without making some pretty important connections. He knows most everyone in government."

"Even in Seattle?" Adam's parents lived in the Boston haven.

Adam shrugged and made a grab for some of the blueberries. "Probably. I'll give him a call and see what I can find out."

I turned the offer over in my head a few times and then nodded. "All right. Can't hurt, I suppose. Although, I would probably avoid mentioning that you're asking on my behalf. Somehow I don't think that would spark much interest."

"Come on, gorgeous." Adam frowned. "I know their visit was a little ... *rocky*, but that doesn't mean they don't like you or wouldn't want to help."

Unconvinced, I held back my reply and dumped another handful of berries into my mouth instead.

Adam laughed and went to rummage through the cabinets for his next snack. I polished off the carton of blueberries—or, at least the ones Adam hadn't swiped for himself—and got up from the table. "You going to be around tonight?"

He turned, his hand clasping a sleeve of crackers. "Sure. Why? You wanna go out for dinner?"

I nodded. "That would be nice. I could use a little break."

"You got it, gorgeous. I promise to keep you completely occupied." Adam grinned but stopped short of giving a full eyebrow wiggle.

I laughed and then crossed the kitchen to give him a quick kiss. "Also, can you feed Boots?"

"Less appealing, but sure."

"Thanks." I strode back to the kitchen door. "I'll see you tonight."

Adam leaned back against the counter and tore open the crackers. "You know, you should take some of Evie's *healthy* cookies to your meeting."

I paused in the doorway. "Why's that?"

"Have you ever tried one?" He flashed a menacing grin. "They taste just like bird food!"

I rolled my eyes. "Do you have much experience with eating bird food?"

"Only when the McNally's dumpster is running low," he said with a shrug.

I shook my head. "I think I'll pass on the cookies."

"Suit yourself but if she gets *peckish*, don't come crying to me."

I groaned. "It's a good thing you're pretty."

Adam chuckled and popped a cracker into his mouth. "See you tonight, gorgeous. Good luck with the bird lady."

I waved and then pushed out of the kitchen, letting the door flap closed behind me.

CHAPTER 10

A little over an hour later, I was seated in Agent Bramble's office waiting for her to return from taking an urgent phone call in the other room. We'd barely begun our discussion before she was called away, and I still wasn't sure of the exact purpose behind her summons. Her office was small, barely large enough for her desk, chair, and a set of filing cabinets. The only drop of personality in the room was a potted plant in the corner but somehow, despite the size, everything was neatly organized and clean. I had no idea where she was keeping all of her supplies, but everything was tucked away out of sight. Not so much as a speck of dust marred the smooth, polished surface of the cherrywood desk.

The office was surrounded by windows and the occupant of the office next door hadn't closed their shades. The neighboring office was roughly the same size as Agent Bramble's and contained the same SPA-issued furniture. That was where the similarities ended. In stark contrast to Agent Bramble's order and neatness, the one next door was a disaster area. Cartons from local eateries littered the desktop, which was completely covered with stacks and piles of paperwork. Two file boxes sat at the edge of the desk, but if there was a system in place, it would be impossible to follow as each of them was stuffed to bursting.

A dark coat hung on the back of the chair, indicating the occupant was somewhere nearby. It looked like the one Agent Mache had worn to the initial interview. If I was Agent Bramble, I would pull the shades on my own side of the shared wall so I wouldn't have to look at the mess all day. I wasn't by any stretch a neat freak, but it was impossible to look at it and not want to snap on a pair of rubber gloves and get to work clearing the clutter.

I was still frowning at the empty office when I sensed movement behind me. I swiveled around in my chair just as Agent Bramble entered the room. Her appearance was just as orderly as her office. Both her fitted tweed skirt and long-sleeved, eggplant blouse were wrinkle-free and looked as though they'd come straight from the dry cleaner. There were spells that could be applied to clothing to render them resistant to stains, wrinkles, stretching, or shrinking; however, those charms were only accessible to the wealthiest of supers. I didn't know the specifics of an SPA officer's salary, but I imagined it wouldn't go very far toward having a witch or wizard enchant your entire wardrobe. Additionally, there was something about Agent Bramble that told me she enjoyed the process of treating her own clothing—that perhaps that's what she looked forward to doing on an otherwise lazy Saturday afternoon.

"I apologize for the delay, Ms. Boldt," she said, taking her seat behind the desk. She reached up and smoothed her long fingers over her tidy bun and then retrieved a large pad of paper from the top desk drawer. She placed it before her and reached back into the drawer for a pen.

"You can call me Holly. If you'd like."

"That's all right," she said. With a click, she lowered the pen to the page and jotted down a few notes. "Now, the main reason I wanted to see you today is in regard to your plans. In order to assign you a new case worker, we need to know what you plan to do now that your temporary banishment has been lifted."

I drew my eyebrows together as I watched her scribble notes. "What about Harvey?"

She lifted her eyes but kept her pen poised against the page. "What about him?"

"Well I mean, is he, has there been—" I stopped and gave a slight shake of my head, refocusing my thoughts. "I assumed this meeting was to talk about his murder."

Agent Bramble straightened and lowered her pen. "Have you thought of any other pertinent details?"

"Uh, well no."

She gave me a confused look. "Then what would there be to talk about?"

I drew in a quick breath and twisted my hands together in my lap. "I want to help. That's all, Agent Bramble."

"We appreciate that, Ms. Boldt. And of course, if there is anything you have to share, we are open to meeting at any time to discuss it. However, for now, that's all out of our hands. It's being investigated to the best of the SPA's abilities."

Right. It was a brush off. Ever so polite, but it stung all the same. Harvey's murder was too personal for me to simply walk away.

"I would like to be kept in the loop," I said forcefully. "We still don't know what that note meant. It could very well have something to do with me. He was with me right before he was poisoned. What if I'm the *ally* it was referring to?"

Agent Bramble plucked her pen up again. "You think you might be a target? Is that what you're saying?"

"I don't know. It all feels a little too strange. The timing, I mean. He was supposed to testify for me and then he gets this mystery call and the next thing we know, he's dead."

"I'm sure that was nothing but an unfortunate coincidence. However, I will pass along your concerns to the agents and officers investigating the case."

There was more I wanted to say—to argue—but Agent Bramble's gaze drifted back to her paperwork.

"Now, back to the topic at hand," she said, starting to write again. "Are you planning to move back to the Seattle haven? Or will you remain in—" She glanced over the papers, her eyebrows furrowed.

"Beechwood Harbor," I supplied.

"Yes." She wrote it down.

"I don't have plans to move back to the haven anytime soon. Without my potions license, it doesn't really make a lot of sense."

She glanced up at the note of disappointment in my voice. "Right."

"My lawyer, Teddy, is trying to get a second hearing, but I'm not getting my hopes up."

She gave a quiet nod. "Probably for the best. I'll put down that you're staying in Beechwood Harbor."

We fell silent as she took down some additional notes. I vaguely wondered what she was writing down. As I waited, my eyes drifted back to the pig sty next door.

"Where's Agent Mache?" I asked her.

"Oh, out *campaigning* for his new job, I'd imagine." There was a sharp edge, almost a bitterness, to her reply but as soon as the words echoed back to her, her dark eyes snapped to mine. "I mean, he's very busy. We all are."

Curiosity uncurled inside my stomach but I ignored it.

Agent Bramble didn't seem like the type who would take kindly to any sort of prodding.

"Remind me what it is you do for work, Ms. Boldt? It says here that you work in a restaurant. Is that still correct?"

I nodded, not bothering to differentiate between a coffee shop and a restaurant. What difference did it really make in the end? As long as I wasn't using magic on the job, the SPA really couldn't care less what I did upon waking each day. I could be a snow cone vendor in the arctic and they wouldn't care. Agent Bramble asked a few other basic questions and then explained that I should have a new case worker assigned to me by the end of the week.

She said goodbye and herded me out of her office. I thanked her for her help and then asked to be pointed toward the nearest restroom. She rattled off the directions and then quickly ducked away, closing the door behind her.

After a quick trip to the restroom, I wove back through the corridors and ended up in the same hallway as her office. The door had been reopened and someone was standing in the doorway, halfway in and halfway out of her office. My footsteps slowed as I neared her open door.

Agent Bramble's voice filtered out into the hall. "—don't think it's proper. It hasn't even been a week! I always knew he was an ambitious man, but this is extreme even for him."

The second voice made a sympathetic noise.

"And before anyone goes around saying I'm jealous, I'm not! I have no desire to take Colepepper's place. This isn't about politics or my estimation of Mache's qualifications. It's a matter of propriety and not looking like we are all a bunch of sharks in the water!"

My eyes widened at Agent Bramble's adamant words. It hadn't even occurred to me that Harvey's death would leave a desirable job vacancy inside the SPA. I only had a fragment of an idea as to the inner workings of the elite office but as I hurried toward the elevator bank, I wondered for the first time if maybe Harvey's killer wasn't motivated by revenge or anger but rather a desire to move up the SPA ladder. Maybe someone had wanted Harvey out of his prestigious office. Permanently.

CHAPTER 11

After leaving the SPA building, I wandered through the haven. I didn't talk to anyone; I simply observed the comings and goings as the afternoon wound down and local restaurants ramped up for the impending dinner rush. As savory scents poured into the streets, I remembered my own evening plans and headed back to the SPA building to use the portal to get back to Beechwood Harbor. I'd been granted permission to use it for the duration of the investigation and planned to use it as much as possible. One step through a doorway and I was transported to the root cellar of a quaint bungalow on Thirteenth Street within the blink of an eye.

Adam was jogging down the stairs when I pushed through the front door of the manor. He was wearing a pair of dark jeans, a navy blue t-shirt, and his signature black leather jacket. He flashed a wide grin at me. "Perfect timing, gorgeous. Hey, would you mind if Evie and Teddy tagged along with us to dinner? Kind of a double date if you will." He wiggled his eyebrows, obviously quite impressed with his own detective skills.

"That's fine," I replied, kicking out of my shoes.

"How was the meeting?"

"Just dandy."

"Holls?"

I glanced over at him. He was sitting on the bottom steps, lacing up his boots. He paused. "What happened?"

"It was a total waste of time. She didn't have any information about Harvey and when I asked, she basically told me it isn't any of my business, which is obviously ridiculous. Of course it's my business!"

"What did she want then?"

"To ask me about my plans for the future. You know, now that I'm only a *mild* social pariah instead of a full-blown fugitive or whatever."

Adam pushed to his feet. "Come here."

I shook my head. "I'm fine. Let me go get changed so we can leave."

Adam sighed but didn't push it as I hurried past him to the hall that led to my room. It was the only bedroom on the first floor—Lacey, Evangeline, and Adam were all housed upstairs. Boots unfolded himself from a pile of clothes on the end of the bed and blinked up at me as I pushed into the room. Normally, he was a miniature bulldozer when I came home, but apparently he'd been too busy napping to bother with it tonight. I stroked his fur and he burst into a loud, rumbling purr. The sound soothed the edges of my frayed nerves and I allowed myself a moment to sit beside him before getting ready.

"I don't even know what's wrong with me, Bootsie." I chewed on my lower lip and stared blankly out the windows that lined the opposite wall. They looked out over the generous side yard, a thatch of pristinely kept grass with a large rose bed that hedged the section of wrap-around porch.

The door that led out to the porch was in the study that adjoined my bedroom. None of us used the study, mostly because Posy liked it when she was in a dark mood, which, to be honest, was the majority of the time. If things were really bad, she'd be in the attic.

"Do you think we should go back to the haven?" I asked Boots, dropping my gaze to the orange fur ball.

He rolled to his back and stretched his expansive stomach into the air.

I rolled my eyes but smiled to myself as I granted his unspoken request for belly rubs. "Oh to have the life of a cat."

His eyes slid shut. Clearly not in a helpful mood.

His purring slowed as he fell back to sleep and I stood to change into a cyan knee-length sweater-dress, black leggings, and a pair of chocolate-colored suede booties. I layered a chunky statement necklace over the cowl neck of the dress, keeping the Larkspur tucked underneath. For a moment, I thought about calling upon Grandmother Honeysuckle. She had recently proved to be useful when I hit bumps or was in full-blown crisis mode. However, regardless of her improved batting average, it still took way too long to cut through her preamble and get to the heart of the advice. I wasn't in the mood to try to pry her off the topic of my love life, not to mention the amount of time it took to gently remind her of my identity every time we spoke.

No, Grandmother Honeysuckle was a last resort and I wasn't quite that desperate yet. Not to mention I now had three people waiting on me for dinner.

I slicked on a layer of lip gloss, freed my auburn from its braid, teased out the soft waves that remained, and went to meet the rest of my dinner companions in the foyer.

Adam looked concerned but I smiled and he relaxed and offered me his elbow. "You look beautiful, Holly."

Evangeline and Teddy smiled at us. "Thanks for letting us tag along," Teddy said, one of his hands going to rest on the small of Evangeline's back. "I think we all need a night out on the town."

Evangeline smiled at her friend—or date—or whatever he was. "Agreed, and Holly, please tell me I can borrow that dress sometime! It's gorgeous."

I laughed. "Of course."

Evangeline was dressed casually—well, casual for her—in a pair of skinny jeans and a bright jewel-tone top that looked even more vibrant against her caramel skin. She always looked amazing in rich or splashy colors.

She and Teddy made an attractive couple. He was wearing a dove-grey three-piece suit, as was his custom. His hair was pushed back from his face with a layer of gel that glistened as he moved under the light from the large chandelier hanging over the foyer. The two of them looked like they should be modeling together in a department store catalog.

Evangeline smiled as Teddy moved her to the door and helped her into a long black coat that reached mid-calf. I tugged on my own coat and let Adam usher me out the door.

"Adam said you went to the haven today?" Evangeline asked as we walked down the steps and toward the sidewalk. McNally's was close enough that it didn't make sense to drive.

"It was a whole lot of nothing," I said. "Agent Bramble is basically playing matchmaker to find me a new case worker and wanted to know what my plans are now that I'm able to return to the haven."

"Oh?" Evangeline gave Adam a curious look. "I didn't want to pry, but what *are* your plans?"

"I don't really know yet. I know I'm not planning to move back to the haven." I stepped onto the sidewalk, careful not to scuff my boots in the gravel. "At least not now."

Adam glanced at me but said nothing.

"Hang in there," Teddy said, offering a reassuring smile. "We'll get a second hearing and get you back on the track you want."

I nodded and tried to return his friendly smile, but it was fleeting.

Conversation faded as we neared the restaurant. Adam held the door open and we all shuffled inside. McNally's is something of a local watering hole and most of the faces gathered around the tables and along the bar were locals. Some offered quiet nods or looks of recognition as we entered. It was strange that a group of supernaturals could blend in so well.

If only they knew ...

I thought back to when Gabriel and I had been together. He'd always been something of an outcast in haven society, which should have been a red flag. However, I'd been an outcast all my life, so it didn't seem so odd to me. The stigma attached to my last name, thanks to my family heritage, was not easy to overcome. I'd never been able to walk around the haven with my head held high, not a care in the world. I'd always secretly worried that people were talking about me behind my back, and it was a given that other witches and wizards were going to judge me as soon as they learned my family name.

It was ironic that the only place where I could finally shrug all that off my shoulders was in a tiny little coastal town made up mostly of humans who had no idea magic was real, let alone knew that several supernatural beings lived and worked in their sleepy community on a daily basis. There was something comforting about living under the radar. It allowed me to truly be the best version of myself. In that light, I wondered why I would ever consider returning to the haven. Why would I want to subject myself to living among those who thought of me as a second-class citizen simply because I'd been born into a notorious bloodline?

Adam took my hand when the chirpy hostess announced that our table was ready. I tucked away the thoughts and smiled, my mind suddenly lighter as we wound through the dining room to a table in the far corner.

Once we were seated, the conversation turned to Harvey's murder and whether or not I'd gathered any more information since the initial meeting with the SPA agents. Teddy was the one most interested in the case and asked a series of questions. "They didn't say anything about the case when you were at headquarters today?"

"Nothing more than the standard boiler-plate speech." I shook my head and used my straw to stab at the slice of lemon bobbing along with the ice cubes in my iced tea. "I got the feeling I wasn't welcome to ask a lot of questions about it. Something strange did happen though." I recounted the snippet of conversation I'd overheard before leaving, as well as the comment Agent Bramble had made about Agent Mache *campaigning* for Harvey's job.

"That was the word she used?" Teddy asked. "Campaigning?"

"Yeah." I tilted my head at him. "It seemed odd somehow."

"Also a little soon," Teddy added as our server delivered our salads.

"What exactly was Harvey's title?" Evangeline asked me. She was delicately picking her way through her house salad, separating the tomatoes from the pile of greens. "I always forget to ask them to leave them off," she added, mostly to herself.

I shrugged. "I never really asked. But I can tell you one thing: from looking at the office spaces alone, it's obvious now that Harvey was somewhere near the top of the food chain."

Evangeline frowned up at me. "I always thought he was ... well I don't know, just a regular agent. Why would you be assigned to such a big wig?"

Adam leaned in conspiratorially and flashed a wicked grin. "Secretly, Holly's a government-sanctioned assassin."

I bit out a laugh. "Right. And my weapons of choice? Plants and pastries?"

"A caffeine-powered super villain!" Evangeline added.

We all laughed, but when it died away it was clear her question remained unanswered. "Harvey was my assigned agent since my parents died. I was just a girl. I'd never given it much thought, but I assume he *was* a normal agent when I was first assigned to him and has since rose in the ranks."

"Maybe, but then why didn't he have you reassigned once he'd risen to the top?" Adam asked before his eyes went wide and he smiled. I didn't even bother turning to look over my shoulder to see what had captured his attention. With Adam it was always one thing: food.

Sure enough, the conversation lulled as the server approached and dished out four entrees.

When she'd gone, I picked up my fork and lifted it over the pile of steaming pasta. "Maybe there's some kind of life-time-appointment rule?"

"I don't think so." Teddy shook his head. "Not that I've ever heard of. There's a whole branch of haven law that deals with disputes between citizens and their assigned caseworkers. It's hard to get a transfer, but not impossible if the grievances are taken seriously enough before the council."

I twisted my lips into a pout. There had certainly been at least a dozen times I'd have liked to explore that option. Although looking back, I was grateful to have been stuck with Harvey, especially now, as I waited to meet whoever would be assigned to me next.

"I guess he just liked you, Holls," Adam teased. "The fiery daughter he never had."

A perfect one second played out before Adam, Evangeline, and I all burst out laughing.

CHAPTER 12

The conversation from the night before continued to play through my mind the following day while I worked my shift at Siren's Song. The amount of clues I had were hardly enough to even form a basic theory on what had happened after Harvey left Council Hall. I still didn't know if he'd ever planned to testify on my behalf. Whatever the reason was for his sudden departure, there were a dozen other questions lurking. Where had he gone immediately after leaving Council Hall? Who had called him away? From the crime scene, it seemed he'd been dosed with poison while inside the cab, but what had he been doing outside the haven? His assistant had confirmed that Harvey wasn't one to leave the haven, yet he'd gone to an off-the-books, last-minute meeting outside the haven, in a cab. None of the pieces made sense individually, let alone when put together. So far, my best guess was that he'd been meeting with some kind of top-secret informant. Maybe in regard to the Praxle case since it was the headlining investigation at the moment? Or had it been someone outside the SPA world? A friend or family member? But then the note found in his pocket didn't make any sense. That was something to do with his role at the SPA. It had to be. But maybe it had been there for days. Maybe he'd simply forgotten about it.

I held each scenario up to the light, twisted it, inspected each angle, but ultimately none of the theories rang true. Particularly depressing was the realization that in all the investigations I'd gotten tangled up in over the past months, I'd always had a partner by my side. It was the first time I didn't have Nick's guidance or advice. He was a former newspaper-reporter-turned-PI and always seemed to have the next three steps mapped out at any given moment. I was sure that if I could share the details of Harvey's case, he would have rock-solid advice for me.

Even if I could find a way to frame it without the supernatural elements, I knew it wasn't a good idea to burden Nick with my problems. Besides, there was no way he wouldn't go digging around trying to figure out what case I was referring to. Would he buy it if I said it was from a TV show?

Thinking about Nick only made me feel worse. Since his unintended stay at the manor, I'd been avoiding him. I didn't know what to say or how to act. He knew me too well. He'd see right through my phony attempts at light conversation while I was really using the entire conversation to mine him for clues as to what parts of the SPA raid he remembered. I wondered if his brush with the supernatural world would ever fully leave him. Part of me wondered if the reason the memory spell hadn't completely taken was because Nick already possessed some sort of inkling that the world around him wasn't quite the way it seemed. If somehow his open-mindedness created a tiny fissure the spell hadn't been able to block. Most humans seemed eager for normalcy. They didn't want to believe, so if they ever encountered something that even hinted at a hidden truth, they would fight until they snapped back to the safety of their familiar world like a rubber band.

"Everything all right, Holly?"

I jumped at Cassie's cheerful voice. I hurried to nod and added a smile for good measure.

She was sweeping near the double doors that led to the back patio but paused and leaned on the broom handle to examine me. Rain streaked down the glass panels and the tables and chairs beyond were soaked from the drizzly day. "You sure? You seem a little out of it today. Still in a post-vacation funk?"

"Something like that I suppose." I shifted my eyes across the room to the front door, wondering if we'd seen our last customer of the day. It was right around the time that Nick usually wandered over to Siren's Song before heading to his condo across town, but Cassie had informed me earlier in the day that she hadn't seen him since I'd taken my vacation.

Cassie resumed sweeping the empty dining room, moving chairs as she went. "Where did you end up going? I completely forgot to ask you the other night when we had dinner. Somewhere with Adam?"

I shook my head and tore my eyes off the front walk outside the small coffee shop. "I went to visit a friend in Seattle."

"Oh, that sounds nice. I haven't been to Seattle in ages. It's odd that it can be so close but somehow out of reach." She smiled to herself. "Maybe I can talk Jeffery into going away for a weekend. In a couple of months, tourist season will be here and I won't have any time."

"That sounds like a good plan. I can always run things here if you want to sneak away for a few days."

"Thanks, Holly. That's really sweet of you."

I ducked my chin in a quick nod. Truthfully, I wasn't sure I should have committed to the offer. After all, things were still up in the air with the case and if Teddy were to somehow finagle a last-minute meeting before the council, I needed to be ready to drop everything and go. Then again, Chief Lincoln, Cassie's boyfriend and town police chief, didn't strike me as the type to do anything on a whim. He'd probably require twelve weeks of planning for something like a weekend away, even if they were only traveling a few hours out of town.

"If you want to add up the tips I can take care of the rest," Cassie said as she rounded the counter. She stashed the broom in the back room and reappeared, dusting her hands off on her apron. "I'm working on ironing out some schedule conflicts so I'll be here late tonight."

"Schedule conflicts?"

She sighed and tucked a loose strand of her chestnut hair back into a low ponytail that was hanging over one shoulder. "Paisley is going to a wedding in Florida and wants a few extra days to bookend the event. Then, at the same time, Kirra needs a few short shifts so she has time to study for a big test she has coming up. I'll figure it out."

"Well let me know if you need me to pick up some extra shifts. I don't mind."

I hadn't told Cassie about my side business going bust. Mostly because that would require saying it out loud, something I wasn't prepared to do just yet.

"I will," she said with a smile.

She went to break down the espresso machine and I turned my attention to divvying up the tip money from the jar standing to the side of the single register on the counter. There were still a few minutes left until closing time, but it was rare for us to have last-minute stragglers. Most days were completely dead for the final half-hour. By the time it was officially closing time, the till was counted, tips were divided, and the espresso machine was cleaned and stood ready for a new day.

Cassie pocketed her tips and said goodbye to me before disappearing into the back office. She'd been getting better at keeping her hours manageable and she had help at home to prepare dinner for her father, who had been disabled in a work accident several years before and couldn't always get around if he was having a particularly painful day. From what she'd told me, she and Chief Lincoln had been spending more time at his place, something she was only able to do since hiring a full-time caregiver to help out at home. Most people around town were betting a proposal wasn't too far away, and for once, I agreed with the gossip mill.

I turned off the Open sign and locked up on my way out. I paused under the awning and looked up and down the street. The rain had let up and I stood for a few moments, mentally weighing my options. I couldn't ignore Nick forever, and if there was a reason he was avoiding me, I wanted to know about it. My mind made up, I hurried across the street and made a quick dash through town to get to Nick's office before the lingering dark clouds let loose again. The log cabin had once been a primary residence for one of the town's oldest families; however, some time ago it had been re-zoned and transformed into a group of cozy offices. Nick ran his private investigator business out of the smallest office in the building, a twelve-by-twelve space at the end of the hall on the first floor. Light shone through his frosted-glass door, so I reached for the handle.

Soft music drifted from the office as I pulled the door open. A bluesy instrumental. Nick looked up when I entered and smiled widely. "Hey there, stranger."

"Hey yourself." I let the door fall closed behind me and

took my place in one of the navy-blue armchairs sitting at an angle before his large oak desk. Nick's office was a perfect reflection of himself. Dark woods and tasteful navy-blue and brass accents lent the space an elegant but unpretentious air. Not a knick-knack out of place, but still casual enough to feel lived in, unlike some offices I'd visited that felt more like a museum or art gallery than a place where work occurred.

"Just getting off work?" he asked after clicking his computer mouse a few times.

"Yeah. I thought I'd stop in and see how you're doing. We've missed you over at the coffee shop."

"I've just been busy." He smiled. "What about you?"

"I'm good." I nodded but immediately felt awkward as silence fell between us. If there was one thing Nick and I were good at, it was talking. When we got quiet, it was sharp and uncomfortable.

I wanted to know if he was still searching for answers regarding the things he saw at Raven, a supernatural nightclub hidden in an abandoned building outside of town, but couldn't quite find a way to bring it up naturally.

"How's business?" I asked instead, hoping to buy some time to find a way to swing things in that direction. His desk was littered with folders I knew contained case notes. He liked to keep paper copies of all his notes, pictures, and other reference items. I leaned forward. "Anything interesting?"

He considered the stacks with a shrug. "One woman hired me to see if I could find the daughter she put up for adoption twenty years ago. The records were sealed so it's been tricky. That's taking up most of my time right now. A few other cases have come and gone."

"I'm glad you're keeping busy."

Nick nodded but his eyes roved over his desk, his mind clearly elsewhere.

"Nick? Is everything all right?"

He glanced up at me. A sudden intensity charged his eyes, making them electric blue. "Have you ever had a repeating dream? The kind you have every night and can't seem to get out of your head?"

My spine stiffened. "I don't think so."

"I've had the same dream every night for over a week now. When I wake up, it's like it's still playing in the back of my mind. I'm starting to lose track of what's real and what's not real." Nick frowned down at his hands, which were folded in front of him on the desk. "You're in it."

"Oh?"

A strange laugh burst from Nick as he realized the connotation of his statement. He held up a hand. "Not anything like that. It's here in town ... well, actually a little outside of town. It's funny, I never paid much attention to that old run-down liquor store on the edge of town but for whatever reason, that's where this whole thing takes place. Somehow it's wedged in the back of my mind."

Dread washed over me and I had to remind myself to breathe. Slow and steady. In and out. Every muscle clenched as I waited for Nick's revelation to continue.

"Then things get ... *weird*."

He looked to me, likely expecting a friendly, curious question, but all my energy was channeled into not gripping the arms of my chair so tightly I'd leave permanent marks in the fabric. I struggled to remain passive, even as my heart thundered frantically, loud enough that it echoed in my ear drums.

When Nick didn't get a reaction out of me, he waved a hand. "Never mind. You don't want to hear about all this."

"No—no—please, finish your story."

I didn't want to know but I had to all the same. It was part of the reason I'd stopped in. Only in hindsight did I realize I wasn't fully prepared to know the truth about his memories of that night. I'd been hoping the meeting would alleviate my conscience, not drag me farther into panic mode.

"Well, there were all these different *creatures*," Nick continued, gesturing with his hand as though he could still see them swarming the parking lot of the liquor store. "Balls of light in all different colors and intensities. Angry men and women with ... fangs."

"Fangs?" I tried to give a lighthearted laugh. "Goodness, Nick. Maybe you should check the expiration date on the cold medicine you've been taking."

He smiled but I could see a flicker of disappointment behind his eyes. He'd wanted something else from me. Some other kind of reaction. "Yeah," he said with a shallow laugh. "Probably should. It's pretty messed up. The other night it changed a little. I was wandering around in your backyard. I thought I saw ... well, I thought I saw a ghost."

"Really?" I said, struggling to keep my voice calm. "What did she—or *he*—look like?"

Nick considered the question for a moment. "Kind of like my elementary school librarian, Mrs. Gilbert."

I tried to laugh but the sound was mangled somehow. Guilt twisted through me, binding my insides into a tight knot. As I watched him, I was suddenly overwhelmed with the urge to come clean. There'd been a few moments over the year since we'd met that I'd wanted to confide in Nick. Stars knew it would be easier than trying to hide everything about myself. If nothing else, it would be nice to let Evangeline loose her cleaning spells after Thanksgiving dinner.

"It's probably the cold medicine. You're right. I'll buy a new bottle on my way home." Nick stared at me for another long moment, as though daring me to correct him. When it was clear I had nothing to add, he pushed up from the desk. He leaned over and clicked a few things on his computer and then started pulling on his thick pea coat. "I suppose I better call it a night. Thanks for stopping by to see me, Holly."

I hurried to get up, feeling even worse at his dismissal. He'd never shooed me out of his office before. He was far too polite to say it, but something shifted in that moment. Almost like he knew the truth and had been setting up a test for me—a test I'd failed miserably.

CHAPTER 13

Back at the manor, Teddy and Evangeline pounced on me as soon as I walked through the door. Before I even had my coat off my shoulders, they were tripping over each other to explain what they'd spent the afternoon working on.

"We've got something to show you," Evangeline started.

"Can we do this in the kitchen? I really need some tea." I turned, hung my coat on one of the pegs beside the door, and tried to pull myself together.

Evangeline nodded and led the way, so wrapped up in whatever they'd been doing that she didn't notice my lack of enthusiasm.

Teddy was more perceptive and sidled up beside me as we crossed through the large living room. "Are you all right?"

I nodded. "Just a long day at work," I lied.

Teddy looked skeptical but didn't press further. He hadn't known me very long, but I imagined working as a lawyer for over a decade made him better at reading people than most.

In the kitchen, Evangeline was already working to spread a selection of glossy papers over the large farm-style table that dominated the eat-in nook to the side of the L-shaped kitchen. I bypassed the table and went to work lighting a burner under my giant ceramic kettle. While I waited for the water to heat up, I added a generous scoop of my favorite soothing blend of tea—made with herbs from the greenhouse—into the largest mug I owned.

"Teddy called a few of his contacts in the Los Angeles haven to see if they have any idea what's going on in Seattle. Turns out Harvey served as the head of the entire crime division in Seattle and was also appointed as the Grand Investigator, which means he had a seat at the table whenever the biggest decisions within the SPA were made. He held one of the top SPA jobs on the entire West Coast."

"Well that explains the fancy office," I said, mostly to myself. I turned and propped myself against the counter as the water in the kettle started to heat up. I eyed the papers she'd fanned out on the table but was too far away to see much more than colorful images and lines of text. Once I'd had a few sips of tea, I'd go closer and investigate. "Have there been any breakthroughs in the investigation?" I asked, not particularly interested in what he used to do at the SPA besides babysit me.

Teddy nodded. He'd positioned his chair at an angle so he could look at both Evangeline and me. "The poisoned coffee was purchased at Magic Beans, the coffee shop that serves as a portal between Seattle proper and the haven."

That caught my attention. "So Harvey left Council Hall, went into Seattle proper via the portal, and got coffee before flagging down a cab?"

"Or he met with someone and they brought the coffee with them," Teddy countered thoughtfully.

"True. Maybe the killer was some kind of informant. Maybe that's why they had to meet outside the haven."

"It's certainly possible," Teddy said. "I know the SPA

works with all sorts of supers to keep a finger on the pulse of the various groups. It's best to be at least one step ahead of the next vampire-werewolf war. Those always get nasty."

"No kidding," I said. "I mean, if Kate Beckinsale can't fix it, what hope do the rest of us have?"

Teddy and Evangeline stared at me blankly.

"Underworld?" I prompted. "Epic vampires vs. werewolves movie."

"Never heard of it," Teddy said.

Evangeline shrugged.

I rolled my eyes. "You guys are from Los Angeles. The home of entertainment."

The water in the kettle was at a rolling boil. I turned my attention to preparing my tea and then joined Teddy and Evangeline at the table. I stood, hovering over Teddy with my cup halfway to my lips as the steam poured off the dark green liquid. As I breathed in the medicinal scent of mint leaves and other herbs and spices, I perused the spread of papers. "So, we don't know who Harvey was meeting. Or why. We also don't know what happened to the driver of the taxi he was found in." I sighed heavily. It seemed there were more blank spots than not. "What are these then?" I asked, gesturing at the pages spread over the tabletop.

"Harriet sent these over. All of these are cases Harvey was involved with that were considered hostile," Evangeline explained. "We got copies of the most interesting ones. As you can imagine, most of the really dangerous supers Harvey helped put away are still serving their sentences. Most will never get out. However, there are a few who have been released."

"Is that Praxle?" I asked, recognizing the smarmy man from *The Witch Wire* coverage.

Evangeline nodded. "If Praxle goes down, he will lose a *lot* of money. Harvey was instrumental in getting his case before the council where other investigations have failed. There are reports of Praxle threatening Harvey in front of other agents."

My eyebrows lifted. "Sounds like motive to me."

Teddy nodded slowly. "The only problem is that he was in his own hearing at the time of the murder."

"He could have hired someone," I suggested.

"I agree that it's worth considering." Teddy reached out and plucked one of the sheets from the collection. "This guy is especially interesting to me."

I looked at the picture in his hand. The face of a shaggy-looking man glared at me from the page. Shifter, if I had to guess. Something large and predatory. A bear? They usually tended to like the gruff, lumberjack look. Some pulled it off better than others. The face staring back at me was less Brawny-paper-towel mascot and more unwashed hermit. "Why's that?"

Teddy's rosy lips twisted into an expression that was a mix between a scowl and a frown. "In my experience, most criminals tend to lay low once they're released from an SPA prison. But this guy, Dune Kasey, he runs right to the press, almost the same day he's released. Says he wants to give a tell-all account that could possibly take down the SPA. Or, my guess, he was hoping to get some kind of settlement for what he claims was mistreatment."

My eyebrows hitched up. "That's ... bold."

Teddy bristled. "Stupid is more like it."

Evangeline smiled at Teddy's response.

"What's his complaint?" I asked.

"He claims he was framed and that even after he presented concrete evidence he was still found guilty."

"And Harvey's connection?"

Evangeline took over. "He had a meeting with Harvey, the lead on the case at the time, and presented his evidence, but three weeks later, Harvey testified against him anyway."

I frowned. "Is that really enough motive to murder someone?"

Teddy looked up at me. "It is when he claims the evidence he presented to Harvey was buried and not presented to the council."

"Hmm. And would it have gotten him off the hook?"

"That's the problem," Teddy replied. "The evidence, whatever it was, vanished. Harvey never put it into the case notes. All it says is that a meeting occurred. Whatever they discussed wasn't recorded."

"Harvey was certainly capable of burying things," I said, frowning.

"Look, all of this might add up to nothing, but it may be worth looking into," Evangeline said.

Teddy nodded in agreement. "Really, at this point, the only thing we know for sure is that there appears to be quite a few people who might have wanted revenge on Harvey."

"Guess being at the top isn't all it's cracked up to be," I said, frowning at the angry faces staring back at me from the pictures. "I'll read through it. Although I'm not sure what I can do even if something does look fishy. Agent Bramble certainly doesn't seem to want my help with the investigation."

Evangeline smiled. "That sounds familiar."

"What do you mean?"

"If you can find a way to work with Chief Lincoln, you can find a way to work with Agent Bramble."

I smiled. "I suppose that's true. Thanks, you guys."

WITCH WAY HOME

THE FOLLOWING MORNING, I got out of bed before the sun was even up. Normally, I despised early mornings. They were a necessary evil of working at a coffee shop. On my days off, I rarely woke before eight-thirty but that morning, sleep was impossible to come by and lying in bed staring blankly at the darkened ceiling was more miserable than facing the prospect of rising before the sun.

My bedroom was freezing cold and I quickly bundled into a thick robe and two pairs of fuzzy socks. Boots stirred on the bed and when I tossed a soft orb of light into the air, I caught a flash of amber eyes staring up at me. "Sorry, Bootsie. Go back to sleep."

His eyes slid closed and I waved a hand to send the light out into the hallway ahead of me. I left the bedroom door open, knowing Boots would want out as soon as he realized I was in the kitchen. I didn't need him yowling and waking up the rest of the household. In the living room, I sent a shower of sparks toward the fireplace and watched as a roaring fire burst to life. The manor had been updated with central heat —a feat Adam claimed had taken months of prodding at Posy —but most of the rooms had a fireplace, and sometimes I preferred the comforting glow of a fire.

While the living room heated up, I padded to the kitchen and made myself a stack of pancakes with sliced fruit, a drizzle of chocolate hazelnut syrup, and a dollop of cream on top. As long as my hands were busy, I was able to block out the knot of worries warring in the back of my mind. When my fit-for-a-gourmet breakfast was ready, I went back out to the living room and plopped myself on the couch before the fire. Posy hated when we ate anywhere but in the kitchen, but she didn't appear to be lurking nearby, so I went ahead. Besides, she'd been sympathetic toward me over the week since the disastrous council hearing and the loss of Harvey.

She'd likely let me get away with it—after a sniff (or twelve) of disapproval.

The luscious scent of my breakfast eventually reached Boots and he waddled into the living room and jumped up to take his place beside me. His pink nose twitched in the direction of my plate and with a long-suffering sigh, I scooped up a dollop of creamy topping and let him lick it off my finger. "There," I told him when he was done. "That's all you're getting from me."

He gave me a long look and blinked his eyes slowly.

I smiled and gave him a second serving. "I don't know how you managed to wrap me so completely around your chubby little paws, but job well done."

He licked happily at the cream and then lay down beside me, wedging his paws under my leg.

"At least you keep me warm," I muttered as I stroked under his chin. "Good for something I guess."

He purred.

After all the work of preparing the picture-perfect breakfast, I scarfed three-quarters of the stack of pancakes before I hit the wall and I couldn't manage another bite. I set the fork aside and balanced my plate on one knee. Footsteps sounded on the stairs behind me and I didn't have to turn to know who it was. "Your food radar appears to be a few minutes slower than Bootsie's," I teased as Adam came around the low-profile couch and sat beside me.

"As long as King Fluff left some for me, I got no complaints." He smiled over my lap at Boots, who was fast asleep. "What are you doing up, gorgeous?"

"Couldn't sleep. Figured I may as well get the day started."

Adam reached for the fork I'd laid to one side and speared three bites of leftovers into his mouth. I passed him the plate and he dug in with typical Adam gusto. "Big plans?"

"I think I might go into the haven and see about meeting

with Harriet, Harvey's assistant. I want to see if she has any information that might be helpful. I'm sure she's already been interviewed, but I want to ask her what she's heard and get her opinion on a couple of cases Teddy and Evangeline brought to my attention."

I'd been up half the night reading the data they'd pulled together. I agreed Dune Kasey seemed to be the most obvious suspect but as far as I could see, there wasn't an address or phone number anywhere in the stack of papers.

"Teddy was also waiting to see if she'd found anything from Harvey regarding my council hearing. I'll see if there's any progress there and offer to help look. All I know is I can't sit in this house waiting another day. If I can't make potions, I can at least help the investigation, and in the process, possibly myself."

Adam polished off the last bite, set the plate on the square coffee table and then draped an arm over my shoulders. "I wouldn't mind a little trip into the haven."

I arched an eyebrow. "Really? You?"

Adam chuckled. "I venture into society every now and again."

"Yes, but not usually voluntarily."

Adam's work occasionally demanded he spend a day or two in Seattle and even within the Seattle haven sometimes. But these trips were usually preceded by lots of complaining and packing procrastination.

"Should we take the train? Or can you still use the portal?"

"No one told me *not* to take the portal anymore." I shrugged. "That's what I was planning to do. Sure beats a three-hour trek."

Adam smiled. "They do have great food on the train though."

I laughed. "Come on. I'll make up the rest of the pancake batter since you've clearly still got food on the brain."

Adam stood and then reached for my hand. I disentangled myself from Boots, who curled into a tighter ball as soon as I was off the couch, and let Adam lead me into the kitchen.

I was halfway through cooking up what was left of the pancake batter when Adam hopped up onto the counter beside me. "So, when are you going to tell me what's on your mind? I don't think I've ever known you to wake up before the sun's even up just for a pancake fix. Is this all because of the case? Or Harvey? Or something else entirely?"

Using the corner of the spatula, I lifted the edge of a fluffy cake. It was the perfect golden brown, so I ignored Adam's question a moment longer and flipped the pancakes over. Once they were sizzling away on the other side, I set aside the spatula and finally risked a peek at Adam. We'd been dating for several months now, and while I was sure we had a lot more to learn about one another, we had the basics pretty well covered. Adam knew when something was on my mind and wasn't content to let me stew in it alone for too long. I supposed it was a good sign of a strong relationship, but there were times when I missed the days when I'd lived alone and could retreat into myself as often and for as long as I needed.

"I think it's a little bit of everything." I sighed heavily and leaned against the counter. "I worked with Cassie last night. She said Nick hasn't been to the shop in over a week, since before I left for my trip."

"Have you seen him? I mean besides that whole fiasco here at the manor?"

I nodded. "I went to his office last night."

"How was he?"

"He said he's been busy, but I think there's more to it. He thinks he's having bad dreams about monsters."

Adam rubbed a hand over the back of his neck. "Oh boy. He's still asking questions about the whole Raven thing?"

I gave a miserable nod. "I got the feeling he knows more than he's letting on. It was almost like he was setting it up, hoping I would confirm his suspicions."

"We've got to figure something out before he makes trouble."

"I know. I just don't have any ideas, or at least none I'm confident enough to try. I don't want to make it worse." I checked the pancakes, my mind churning. "I don't think he would say anything to anyone else. At least we have that in our favor. The SPA isn't going to catch wind of some human talking about a supernatural sighting." I chewed on my lower lip for a moment. "At least, I don't think so."

That was the last thing I needed—another SPA scandal within Beechwood Harbor. There'd been more close calls than I cared to admit since my arrival in the sleepy little town. What can I say? Trouble follows me around like a hungry stray cat follows a fisherman.

"I don't think he would say anything to someone he didn't trust, and from what I can see, his only friends are here in this house," Adam said.

I smiled up at him. "Are you saying Nick is your friend?"

Adam rolled his eyes.

"Aww. That's adorable!" I giggled and served up a plate of pancakes. "And also, it's about time!"

He took the plate, dropped a quick kiss to my lips, and then sauntered to the table. "I didn't say we were going to start hanging out or anything," he groused.

I tucked my smile away but held onto the warm feeling that remained. Nick and Adam had been rivals for far too long. I suspected it had more to do with some perceived threat on Adam's part because he'd originally worried Nick was a competitor for my attention. However, the tension remained long after Adam and I started dating. I wasn't sure when Adam had changed his mind, but I was glad he had finally come around. Now if I could just get him to stop baiting Lacey.

Right. Piece of cake. About as easy as telling a lion to eat a salad.

CHAPTER 14

The rest of the household was stirring to life as Adam and I headed for the door. We passed a sleepy-looking Evangeline as she padded down the stairs, wrapped in an exotic silk robe that fell to her ankles. Teddy was a few steps behind, rubbing his eyes. I smiled at the way his boyish blonde hair was sticking out in every direction. It was a far cry from his usually polished, three-piece-suit exterior. He'd been staying in the guest room at the very end of the hall during his stay, but I hadn't seen him in his full morning glory.

We exchanged goodbyes at the foot of the staircase and then Adam and I headed out. The morning air was brisk but once we started walking, it wasn't too bad. The portal to the haven was less than a mile away and within half an hour, we'd crossed from Beechwood Harbor to the hustle and bustle of the haven streets. Shops and restaurants were already in full swing. Smells of coffee and pastries poured out from a local café and Adam started drifting toward the front doors. I laughed at the way his stomach steered him, but followed him inside anyway. We had espresso and split a basket of freshly baked muffins in front of the picture window and people-watched as the citizens of the haven started their days.

As we left the shop, I muttered that I really needed to restart my gym membership.

Nick's memory problem was still in the front of my mind as we walked toward the SPA building in the heart of the haven. We passed a small potion shop and I got an idea. I tugged Adam's coat sleeve and we ducked inside just as the shop owner was unlocking the front door. He was a stocky man and wore a long robe, the traditional attire for potions masters. He welcomed us to his store and told us to let him know if we needed anything special.

Adam started to the right and I followed a step behind, my eyes roving the store, trying to take it all in. In some ways, it reminded me of Mrs. Clairmont's shop—the one that had been tangled up in the awful business with Bill Praxle. I wondered what this shop owner would say about the whole mess. I considered him as he bent over a ledger. He seemed friendly enough, but I knew I'd only get one shot, one chance to wheedle information out of him. It wouldn't look good if I assaulted him with a laundry list on inquiries so I had to choose carefully.

I tapped Adam's arm and gestured that I was going to speak to the wizard. He nodded, then went back to perusing a section of gleaming bottles, each a variant of neon orange. The label on the counter in front of them identified the potion as an instant cure for nausea. I smiled and shook my head to myself as I started toward the counter. Adam had a reputation for rummaging through the dumpsters of local restaurants when in his beast form. I had no doubt he often shifted back and found his human system rebelling against the ridiculous amounts of spoiled food he'd stuffed himself with during his run as a dog. He'd likely walk out with a case of the orange concoction.

The wizard at the counter glanced up as I approached. "Is there something I can help you with, Miss?" he asked with a broad smile.

He was nothing like the potions master I'd worked for when I'd lived in the haven. Mr. Keel had been surly and argumentative—even with customers. It was no surprise that he'd been forced to close his business just months after my arrest.

"I don't know a lot about potions," I said, starting from a position that I hoped would allow me to wring the most information from him. "What I'm looking for might not even be possible..."

He gave an encouraging smile. "Well, why don't you tell me what you need solved and I'll find a way to help."

"Thank you." What a refreshing wizard. "I'm wondering what you would recommend for someone who would like to block out memories."

The wizard's smile faltered slightly. "I'm not sure I understand, Miss."

"Like, for example, someone who experienced a trauma," I said, hoping I wasn't coming across as someone cooking up some terrible scheme. I gave a nervous smile and leaned in closer. "I can't really give away the details, but I have a friend who's been through something she would rather forget. Permanently."

The wizard's eyes flashed with recognition. I had no idea what scenario he'd conjured up in his mind, but whatever it was, it seemed to serve my purpose because he held up a stumpy finger. "I see. One moment please."

He ducked into the back room of the shop and I took a moment to look over his work space. Potions masters did most of their work behind closed doors because potion making was a rare gift and was closely guarded and cloaked in secrecy. However, there were occasions when someone would request a special customization and potions masters would oblige right there on the spot and make some kind of alteration. This shop keeper was extremely neat and tidy; there wasn't a trace of the prior day's work on his counter. The ledger he'd been working on showed neat rows of figures and from the short glance I took, it looked as though business was drying up slightly. Each day appeared to have fewer and fewer sales as the month had wandered on. Once again, I wanted to ask him about the Praxle fiasco.

He returned moments later with a vial that contained a silver liquid that almost looked like mercury in the way it swirled and moved inside the container. "This is a memory potion that can temporarily alleviate unpleasant memories."

He passed me the vial and I tipped it one way and then back again, mesmerized by the way it moved. "What are the ingredients?" I asked, wondering if I'd be able to guess them as he listed them off. Some kind of potion nerd challenge.

"The base is a syrup made from distilled hyssop. Then there are a number of herbs added to that base. Most prominently hydrangea root and juniper bark."

"Hydrangea root and hyssop? Is that wise?" I lifted an eyebrow and watched the rippling liquid as I rolled the vial between my fingers. "Aren't you worried about the interaction?"

The wizard was studying me with a wary look. "I thought you said you didn't know much about potions?"

Bat wings.

Potion work was instilled in me so deeply I hadn't even thought twice before blurting out my concerns.

I smiled sweetly and gave a little shrug. "I know a *few* things." It was an absurdly thin cover-up. While most witches and wizards knew basic botanical ingredients, knowing the interactions between different plant elements was far from common knowledge.

The wizard gave a slow, unconvinced nod. "It's a temporary solution. As I'm sure you know," he continued coldly, "mind magic is extremely advanced and is better suited to spell work rather than potions."

"Right." I frowned and set the vial down on the counter to fish out my wallet. "How does this work?"

"The first time the potion is dispensed, the person—your *friend*—must be focusing on the memories they would like banished. Then, consume one drop. That helps the potion bind to those specific memories. After that, the maintenance dose is a single drop every day. It's available in a capsule formula. Some people prefer that as they can simply sneak it in with their daily vitamins and not be forced to dwell on the reason for taking it. Eventually, say after a week or so of consistent use, the memories will be hidden deep enough that they won't surface even if the next day's dose is off by an hour or so. Of course, the biggest problem with this type of potion is that at some point the user forgets why they even have it and stop taking it altogether."

"Right …," I tried to mask the disappointment in my voice. I'd been hoping for something far less complicated. Even if I could find a way to give Nick the first dose while he was consciously focusing on the night of the raid, there was no way I would be able to slip him a drop or pill every day at the same time for the rest of his life.

"If the potion is stopped abruptly the results can be disastrous."

"How so?"

"The bound memories build and build and come rushing back in a way that is far more damaging than if they're dealt with gradually, over time. Almost like a monsoon after a dry spell."

I cringed.

The potions master picked up the vial. "Would you still like to try it?"

I considered the silver liquid and then shook my head. "I'm not sure it would work for what I need."

The wizard slipped the vial into the pocket of his robe. "It's certainly not a hot seller," he conceded. He glanced around the shop, his eyes tracking Adam for a moment before he leaned in closer. "My advice would be to tell your friend to seek out someone who is experienced with mind magic. You'll have to look carefully. As I'm sure you know, it's frowned upon and not something advertised in the Herald. Just be careful, Miss. There are a lot of crooks out there."

"Right. Well thank you anyway. I appreciate your time."

He nodded and ducked back into the back room. I sulked by myself for a minute, then rejoined Adam. He was inspecting a series of potions that looked similar to the line of hair products Evangeline and I had created for her to sell at her day spa. Adam had a head full of dark locks and took them very seriously. He glanced over at me and held up a bottle. "You and Evie should try to sell your stuff here," he said. "Your packaging is better by a mile, and get a whiff of this stuff." He held out the bottle. "It smells like something I would find to roll in out in the forest."

I wrinkled my nose and gingerly accepted the bottle. I'd already decided that if Adam and I ever cohabitated, he would be responsible for his own post-shift laundry.

I took the bottle and sniffed at the contents. Adam laughed when I recoiled. "Bat wings! What in the Otherworld is in this?" I twisted the bottle, looking for a list of ingredients, but nothing was listed. I'd picked up the habit from living in the human world where everything was neatly labeled. I'd forgotten that in the haven it was rare to

WITCH WAY HOME

find specifics like that. Apparently labels ruined the *mystique*.

Adam took the bottle back and set it on the shelf. "Should we go? What time are you meeting Harriet?"

I started to answer but was interrupted by the melodic chime of the door opening. The potions master appeared from the back with a wide smile for his new customer. "Morning, O'Doul," he called out brightly.

I glanced over my shoulder but didn't recognize the tall man who walked in. He had the stately walk of someone important and I immediately decided he was a wizard. In the haven, those with the most pomp were wizards and witches, who were, for better or worse, at the top of the pecking order in the supernatural community. They'd founded the council, written the laws, and were the ones responsible for the creation of the hidden worlds locked behind the safety of the intricate and powerful charms and enchantments that keep the supernatural population hidden in plain sight in major cities all over the world. It was impressive, but I'd never quite related to the air of superiority that some exuded like cheap perfume.

"Brought your paper in," the tall wizard said, handing it over the counter to the shop owner. "Look who's front page news again."

I watched the shop keeper's reaction, surprised when a snarl marred his kindly face. "He's lucky he's locked up in SPA custody or I'd hunt him down myself."

I glanced at Adam. He didn't appear to be paying attention but I knew him well enough to know his ear was perked in their direction.

"Trust me, there's a lot of us who will be after him, wands blazing, if he manages to wiggle his way out from under the council's wrath," the tall wizard said.

"I don't know if things here will hold until then," the

DANIELLE GARRETT

potion master said quietly. "Things are in a complete free-fall right now. I've slashed prices as much as I possibly can, but I can't compete with the cheap garbage they've flooded the market with."

"I know. It's an all-too-common story. Hilda Clairmont was in my office a few days ago. The shop where she'd been selling her potions since this whole mess started has canceled over half the orders they've placed. Said they weren't moving enough of them to keep up that pace."

"Poor Hilda."

"Shame about Colepepper too."

My heart leapt into my throat.

"Yes. After all the hard work of getting this case before the council, he won't be here to see the fruit of his efforts." The potions master cleared his throat. "I appreciate you bringing this by. Let me go get your order."

The tall wizard thanked him and wandered to the opposite end of the store to browse while the potions master disappeared into the back room yet again.

Adam took my elbow and steered me toward the door. As we passed the front counter, I glanced over and caught the headline and accompanying picture on the Haven Herald:

PRAXLE CASE HEADS INTO DAY EIGHT. WILL THERE BE A VERDICT?

Underneath was a shot of a smarmy-looking businessman. His dark hair was slicked back mobster-style and he held a thick cigar between two slender fingers. He was grinning as though he's just shared a dirty joke with the person wielding the camera. A sick feeling curled in the pit of my stomach and my skin crawled; I was grateful when Adam led me out of the shop and I could get a breath of fresh air.

CHAPTER 15

At half past eleven, I was sitting in the lobby of Harvey's office, waiting for Harriet to get off the phone. She looked like she hadn't slept for days. Her eyes were rimmed with red, and her skin had a gray pallor and lacked its usual rosy hue. I'd been waiting for nearly half an hour. Her phone was ringing off the hook but she'd promised that if I could hang around a little longer, she had a replacement coming in to take over for her. Eventually, a petite woman with sleek black hair, square-rimmed glasses, and a pert nose sashayed into the office and relieved Harriet. The two women exchanged soft words and then Harriet grabbed her purse and headed away from the reception desk.

"I'm sorry, Holly. Things here have been crazy."

I inclined my head. "I can imagine. How are you holding up?"

She shrugged but her eyes glossed over and she blinked rapidly to clear the unshed tears before they could slip down her cheeks. "It's different here without him. He drove me mad sometimes, but now I find I miss those moments the most."

"I'm so sorry, Harriet," I said, reaching for her hand.

She smiled softly. "I imagine you can relate."

"Yes," I replied with a quiet laugh. "It always felt like we were on opposite ends of the table. But now, looking back, I can see it all a little more clearly."

Harriet wiped at her eyes. "Would you like to get a coffee? I have half an hour if you'd like. I wasn't sure exactly what you wanted to discuss. I know your lawyer is hoping for some kind of notes or documentation as to what Harvey planned to say in his testimony at the council hearing, but I'm afraid I haven't been able to find anything yet."

"Thank you for looking. I would certainly appreciate anything you can find, but that's actually not why I'm here." I looked past her shoulder to where her replacement was now fielding the firestorm of phone calls and felt a guilty pang. "I should have called ahead."

She waved off my apology. "Don't worry about it. Come on; there's a cafe on the first floor where we won't be disturbed. It's the kind of place where everyone minds their own business."

I smiled. "That must be nice. I can't think of a place in Beechwood Harbor where people aren't listening in on everything. Gossip is the lifeblood that keeps the town running."

Harriet returned my smile and led the way to the elevator in the center of the building. SPA headquarters was a strange clash of the past and the present. The offices themselves were stately and held a certain old-world charm. The SPA didn't use computers or internet databases for record keeping or data storage. Instead, everything was written down and meticulously stored in a complicated filing system that required a horde of assistants to keep orderly.

Wards were applied to documents to maintain the security of information and agents had to be of a certain security level to release them. It was a system that worked similarly to the FBI. Clearance levels were assigned to specific supers and only they were able to access more sensitive information. It worked well, had for hundreds of years, but after spending so much time in the human world, it was a stark contrast to the technology-obsessed culture I now lived in. Even the oldest citizens of Beechwood Harbor would be lost without their smart phones and home computers.

"Do you like living with the humans?" Harriet asked as we stepped onto a waiting elevator. They were powered by magic and were virtually silent, lacking the shudder and swoop of mechanical elevators. That was one area where the haven had the upper hand. I could still remember the first time I'd ridden in a human elevator. I thought the other passengers were going to have to peel me off the ceiling before we'd even ascended a single floor.

"I do," I replied with a nod. The doors slid closed and we glided down to the first floor with hardly a quiver. "I didn't think I would. Before Harvey sent me away, I'd only ventured into the human world on a handful of occasions. But now, after a year away, it almost feels like culture shock to come back to the haven. I hadn't expected that."

The doors slid open and a cluster of supers moved aside to let Harriet and me out before they piled into the empty shell. Harriet pointed and I followed her to a quaint cafe around the corner from the elevators and the main entrance of the SPA headquarters. She explained that most of the patrons were agents and other SPA employees, but it was technically open to the public. When we wandered inside, there were a few groups of people gathered around tables, talking in low voices. A mild, folksy tune played over the sound system. Two employees behind the counter hopped to attention as we approached.

Harriet ordered a sandwich and an iced tea. I copied her

order, momentarily wondering if I should order something to take with me for Adam. He'd gone off to visit a few of his favorite haven shops while I met with Harriet. She didn't know Adam and I figured she'd be more open if it was just a one-on-one visit. The cashier rang up the purchase and Harriet handed over three coins. I tried to pay for my portion but she insisted. Moments later, food in hand, we took a place at a small table in the corner farthest from the other groups of customers.

"I know we don't have much time, Harriet, so I'll cut right to the chase. I wanted to meet with you today to see what you can tell me about Harvey's case. No one will tell me much of anything and I wanted to know if there have been any developments. I met with Agent Bramble a few days ago. I don't know for sure, but it felt like there was something she wasn't telling me."

Harriet picked up her sandwich and considered it for a moment. "I don't know how much help I'll be. To be honest, they aren't telling me much, either. They are keeping the whole thing quiet. Almost ... *too* quiet."

I paused. "Do you think they might suspect it's someone on the inside of the agency?"

Harriet looked up, bug-eyed.

I glanced to the left and right, checking that we were far enough away from the other diners that I wouldn't be overheard. When I was sure it was safe, I leaned in and told her what Agent Bramble had said about Agent Mache. Harriet didn't look surprised.

Instead, she sighed. "He's been after Harvey's job for some time. The two of them used to work together, actually. Not a lot of people remember that. Agent Mache looks a lot younger than he really is. He and Harvey were partners when they were both fresh to the job."

"Partners?" I certainly hadn't expected that.

"Not by choice. They were forced to work together but there was no love lost between them. Everyone knew they despised one another. Eventually, their career paths took them in different directions. Harvey was promoted to General Investigator. He was in charge of special operations and running task forces. The big, headline assignments. Meanwhile Agent Mache was assigned to the supernatural crimes division, which isn't quite as glamorous."

I nodded, the pieces shifting and fitting together in my mind.

"Agent Mache doesn't agree with a lot of the policies Harvey put into place and was becoming more and more vocal about his opposition. His behavior following Harvey's untimely death has actually been quite shocking to most of us. Normally you would expect time to mourn and grieve before someone else comes in demanding attention. Whether or not he agreed with Harvey, it doesn't seem right to be so outspoken about him when it hasn't even been two weeks since his death."

"That must be ruffling some feathers," I said, remembering a moment too late that Agent Mache's partner, Agent Bramble, was an eagle-shifter. Why couldn't I get away from the bird metaphors?

Harriet didn't seem to notice the unfortunate choice of words. She nodded her head. "No one is happy about it and if you ask me, it's having the opposite effect than he wanted. He's getting attention but it's not the right kind. To be frank, he is coming across as quite heartless. While there are situations where being tough and resilient are admirable qualities, when it comes to the passing of one of our own, it doesn't sit right."

"Do you think he wanted Harvey out of the way enough to …" I let my words trail off, but the implication was clear.

If my question scandalized her, she didn't show it. Harriet

hurried to shake her head. "I don't think so. I mean, Agent Mache is a hot-head but I don't think he's a killer."

"What about Harvey's other enemies? What can you tell me about Dune Kasey? He's been making the news lately."

Harriet considered her plate for a moment. When she looked up at me, her expression was twisted, almost pained. "Harvey was right about you," she started. "Your instincts are very sharp."

For some reason, her words choked me up. A lump rose in my throat and I reached for my iced tea, hurrying to sip some down, and then coughed quietly into my napkin.

"I told the investigators but I'm not sure how seriously they took me," she said. "Over the weeks since Dune's release from prison, Harvey received some threatening letters. They were never signed and came via an untraceable messenger bird. He brushed them off as nothing to worry about, but I always had a weird feeling about them."

"You think they were from Dune?"

"The timing fits."

"That does seem like too much of a coincidence. Did you hand the letters over to the investigators?"

Harriet nodded. "They took them, but like I said, I'm not sure how much weight they gave to them."

"Did you know they found a note in the car with Harvey?"

"Yes. They showed me a picture of it. The handwriting was the same."

I leaned back in my chair, all interest in my lunch gone. "And they aren't taking that seriously?" It was a bewildering thought. "I can't imagine a more direct clue!"

Harriet shot a glance around and I regretted raising my voice. The last thing I wanted to do was spook her. "The notes never threatened violence," she clarified. "They were mostly vague threats. Like the one in the car: *choose your allies carefully.*

"Does that sound like something Agent Mache would say?" I asked, merging the two theories together in my mind.

Harriet considered the question for a long moment before finally shaking her head. "I don't think so. And even if it was, why would he send anonymous letters? He wasn't exactly shy about making his opinions loud and clear as often as possible to anyone who would listen."

I nodded slowly, turning the theory around to see if I could find another angle. "What if they were meant to intimidate Harvey? Maybe the author thought they would scare him out of the job?"

Harriet shook her head. "Anyone who knows Harvey knows he's made of steel." She paused and her face fell. "Was, I suppose."

Harriet had stopped eating her meal after the first few bites. The clock was winding down on our time together.

"Can I ask you one more thing?"

"Of course," she said.

"When Harvey was assigned to be my case worker, he was still at the beginning of his career with the SPA. Clearly he rose quite high in the ranks in the years since. Why did he stay on as my assigned agent? Why didn't he ever foist me off onto some lower-level agent?"

Harriet gave a watery smile. "He liked you, Holly."

It was a simple answer but had the force of a knockout punch. I nodded but then scrambled to my feet and went to the counter to ask for a couple of take-out boxes. We packaged up our leftovers in silence. I put a few coins on the table—haven currency—and led the way back to the door. As we walked out into the expansive lobby, I realized I hadn't asked Harriet for advice regarding my chances at getting a second council hearing. As I turned back to ask her, my gaze snagged on someone across the lobby. Ben, the masseuse who worked for Evangaline, was standing at the reception counter, off to one side like he was waiting for someone. I raised a hand to see if I could catch his attention, but quickly snapped it back against my side as a woman with long, dark hair and a cold smile joined him.

My heart gave one loud *thump* and then stopped for a couple of beats.

I reached out, blindly pawing for Harriet. "Harriet—Harriet, who is that woman over there? With the long hair in the purple suit."

"Ugh. That's Sasha Pringle," Harriet answered, her nose wrinkled in disgust. "Do you know her?"

I shook my head. "No, but she sure seems to have some strong opinions about me. She was on the council for my hearing."

"Oh."

I glanced at Harriet. I was about to ask her what she knew about Sasha but she was consulting the watch on her wrist. "I'm sorry, Holly. I would love to stay and talk, but I told Si I would be back at one."

"Thank you for meeting with me today," I said. "I'll stop by and say hello next time I'm in the haven. Maybe we could have lunch again under better circumstances."

"I'd like that, Holly. You take care of yourself. Harvey would have wanted that."

I nodded and gave her a quick hug. She shuffled back toward the elevators and I ducked behind one of the columns and watched as Ben and Sasha untangled from an embrace. My heart slammed frantically in my chest as a million questions exploded in my mind.

My phone chirped and I nearly jumped out of my skin. It was a text from Adam, saying he was holding a table for us at a restaurant around the corner from SPA headquarters. I glanced back at Ben and Sasha as they headed for a set of doors on the other side of the lobby, then made a run for the nearest exit.

Sasha Pringle. I had a name. The witch who was bent on destroying my career was no longer a mystery woman lurking in the shadows. She was front and center, and I was going to figure out what her problem was, then get her out of my way.

CHAPTER 16

"What happened to you?" Adam asked as I burst into the restaurant, fuming mad.

"Sasha Pringle," I huffed, plopping into the seat Adam pulled out for me.

He sank into his own chair and frowned. "Sasha Pringle? Who is that?"

"The witch who's trying to ruin my life!"

"Okay, slow down," he said, holding up one hand.

"Did you ever ask anyone about her?"

Adam looked around and then leaned in a little closer. The restaurant was in the middle of the lunch rush and there were occupants at both of the tables beside us. "I got a list of witches who serve on the council and was digging into each of them. The name Sasha rings a bell, but I couldn't tell you much about her. At least not yet."

"Well, she's at SPA headquarters and she wasn't alone. She was with Ben!"

"Ben?" His thick eyebrows wrinkled together. "Evie's Ben?"

"Yes!" I barked. "How many Bens do we know?"

Adam scowled. "There's no need to get snippy."

I forced my hands to unclench. "You're right. I'm sorry. It's just—she's so—" I stopped myself and drew in a slow breath. "It startled me. Seeing her like that."

Adam's expression softened, the irritation ironed out. "I wonder how she knows Ben."

"I have no idea, but I'm definitely going to find out. If they're friends, maybe Ben can tell me just exactly why she hates my guts so much."

"You think Ben would help?"

Magic tingled in my fingertips and I swallowed hard. "I'll find a way to convince him."

"Holly…"

I ignored his would-be warning and started crafting the speech I'd give to Ben in order to get him to help me. I didn't know him very well, but Evangeline might have some insight that could help me find his soft spots.

Adam ordered lunch for himself and I picked at the French fries on the plate, mindlessly nibbling on them as I scanned the streets beyond the large cafe windows. The haven was a big place but I was convinced Sasha and Ben were going to go waltzing by at any moment. When Adam finished and paid the tab, we bundled back into our coats and headed out. We'd need to go back to the SPA building if we wanted to use the portal back to Beechwood Harbor. My senses kicked up another notch as we hurried down the street toward the glittering building.

"Hold on," I said, stopping in front of a corner store. I scooped a Haven Herald from the bin outside the shop's doors and ducked inside to pay for it. I wanted to read the article the two wizards had been discussing that morning in the potion shop.

"It's been forever since I've had one of these," I said once I rejoined Adam on the sidewalk. "Why don't we have a subscription delivered to the manor?"

"We used to," he answered.

"What happened?"

Adam grinned. "A couple of years ago, we had a temporary guest at the manor. They'd arranged to stay for six weeks. Some kind of shifter—he didn't talk much. We all figured he was just the shy type. Two weeks after he checked out, a piece came out in the Herald that told the story of the manor and the history of the inhabitants. It turned out his entire stay had been some kind of research trip and he'd been mining us all for a newspaper story. Posy was furious."

I grimaced. "Did the roof have to be replaced afterward?"

Adam chuckled. Posy's soul was linked to the manor and when her emotions fluctuated too strongly, the manor itself reacted in her stead. "The manor remained intact, but she refused to come out of the attic for a few weeks She stayed up there stewing. When she finally came back down, she announced we would no longer have the Herald and demanded that one of us cancel the subscription."

"And that was that," I said with a shake of my head.

Adam pointed at the paper in my hands. "So you're going to have to smuggle that thing inside and if I were you, I'd stash it under the bed until you can recycle it."

I laughed and tucked the paper under my arm. "Noted."

Adam didn't seem to notice my apprehension as we neared the SPA building. He pulled his cell phone out of his pocket—a flashy gadget with a shiny silver case. How he managed to walk and type on the small screen at the same time was beyond me. I didn't ask, knowing he'd give me some "it's a shifter thing" reply. After a few blocks, he swiveled the phone around to face me. "That her?"

I nodded at the image of Sasha Pringle staring back at me. "How did you find that?"

Haven society didn't use the internet. The *Witches Web* was the closest thing and it worked more like a catalog service to order supplies from inside the haven and have them sent by carrier bird or courier to outside cities. Most magic wielders found themselves in a constant war with technology; therefore, the Haven Council had deemed the internet to be useless.

Adam grinned at me. "Believe it or not, the havens are moving into the twenty-first century, bit by kicking-and-screaming bit. It's all very hush-hush right now, but someone high up on the totem pole in the council contacted one of the companies I freelance for to see about getting basic information put onto a website. I think they're tired of supers nagging them about it. Just because most witches and wizards are technophobes doesn't mean the rest of us shouldn't have a database of haven information available at our fingertips."

I frowned at him. "Are you including me in the former camp?"

He shrugged. "You're a witch. I've never seen you use your phone for anything besides phone calls and texting. I don't even think you have an email account."

I wanted to object just on principle for being lumped into a catch-all category, but he had me pegged.

Adam gave a good-natured laugh and wrapped an arm around my waist. He pulled me closer to him. "That's okay, gorgeous. It just means you have one more reason to keep me around."

I rolled my eyes but couldn't help smiling at him. "What does it say about the ever-so-lovely Ms. Pringle?"

Adam read from the screen. "Sasha Pringle. Born to Winston Jarvis and Marla Pringle—"

"Bat wings! Winston Jarvis? As in *Councilman* Jarvis?"

Adam nodded. "Guess so."

"No wonder she's got a seat even though she looks barely older than me. Daddy must have swung that for her." Within witch and wizard families, it was the mother who passed on their family name to their offspring. It made sense that I—and likely a whole lot of other supers—hadn't made the connection to Councilman Jarvis.

"There's not a lot about her listed here, but this system is all new. More information will be added in the coming months." Adam scanned his finger up and down the screen of his phone. "Says she's been on the Seattle Haven Council for two years. It doesn't give the specifics of the cases she's presided over, so we can't figure out if there's a connection there."

"At least not without going to the records office and requesting the files," I added.

"Guess we know what Teddy's going to be doing," Adam teased.

I nodded but wondered if it might be just another waste of time. Without Harvey's testimony, it would be all-too-easy for the council to rule against me whether or not Sasha Pringle was on it.

"I just want to know why she hates me so much," I said after a minute. "You should have seen her, Adam. She was ready to attack me right out of the gate. She was like a boxer in the ring or something. I've never met her or her parents as far as I know. Why would she act like that?"

Adam turned off the screen and pocketed his phone. "I don't know, gorgeous. We'll get to the bottom of it though. I promise you that." He kissed the side of my head and then moved to open the door of the SPA building.

~

We headed back to the manor and as soon as we made it

inside—after a brief attack by Boots—I hurried through the house, going from room to room looking for Teddy. I wanted to let him know what we'd found out and see if there was any way he could go to the records office and petition to see what Sasha Pringle's history was like. Maybe we could see if there was some kind of connection. Did she always fight so hard against cases like mine, or was it personal somehow? It would be more helpful to speak directly with other council members, but there was a certain level of secrecy among them. Even if there are disagreements, they weren't likely to discuss that with anyone outside of law enforcement.

As I was hurrying back for the top of the stairs, Posy floated through the ceiling directly below the attic. She shimmered and then her translucent form solidified ever so slightly. She gave me a polite smile. "Hello dear."

"Hello, Posy. Have you seen Evangeline or Teddy today?"

She shook her head. "No one has been here all day. Well, other than Lacey of course."

"Okay. Thanks."

"Is everything all right, dear?"

"Yeah. I just wanted to talk to him about a development with my petition to the council."

Posy nodded. "How are you doing? I know how important potions are to you."

I shrugged one shoulder, surprised by the swell of emotions her question dragged up. "I'll figure it out."

"I'm sure you will, dear." She smiled, but it was clear my tough-witch act wasn't fooling anyone. Without another word, she floated through the floor to the first level of the manor. Boots rammed his head into my leg and I bent to scoop him from the floor. I talked softly to him as I headed back downstairs.

Adam was on the couch, flicking through something on his phone. His expression was pinched and distracted.

"Everything okay?" I asked, joining him on the couch. Boots sprawled out of my arms and lay across both of our laps. I smiled as I stroked my fingers through his thick, tawny fur. He and Adam hadn't always been the best of friends but since we'd started dating, Boots had decided he wasn't all bad.

Adam glanced over at me. "Yes and no. Work stuff."

"Oh."

"What are your plans for the rest of the day?"

I stifled a yawn. The sleepless night was catching up to me. "I don't have anything in the fridge. I've been avoiding the grocery store since I got back."

"Tell you what—you run out and get groceries, I'll get this work stuff off my plate, and we can call it an early night and watch a movie or something."

I agreed, then headed into town to get groceries at Thistle while Adam checked in with work. He worked for himself and could set his own work schedule, but there was inevitably going to be a slush pile of emails waiting for him after only a few hours away from his desk.

On my way back, gripping the handles of two canvas grocery bags, I took a detour and stopped in at The Emerald. Evangeline and Lucy were at the front desk and both glanced up when I walked in. "Holly! I didn't know you were back from the haven," Evangeline said.

"Hey guys." I set my grocery bags on one of the plush chairs near the door and made little circles with my wrists to get the circulation flowing again. As always, I'd ended up with way too much food for the two bags but stubbornly insisted on making it all fit. The result was two extremely heavy bags that were going to make the trek up the hill back to the manor a pain. "I just got back a little while ago."

"Anything to report?" Evangeline asked.

"Yes and no. Nothing solid yet. I'll keep you posted." I glanced around the shop. "What time is Ben coming in today?"

Evangeline sighed. "I'm not sure. He's at a doctor's appointment."

Lucy frowned at her. "He's cutting it pretty close getting back. His client is already here waiting. It's the third time in the last week. I hate to say it, but I think it's going to cause problems."

Evangeline nodded but from the look on her face, it was clear she didn't want to deal with it.

I supposed Ben *could* have been at a doctor's appointment, but then why was he at the SPA building, tangled up with Sasha Pringle? I wasn't sure how to go about asking for information, but I planned on confronting him next time I saw him.

I stretched back, working out the tensed muscles in my arms and shoulders, and spotted a glittery new display on the front counter to the right of Evangeline. I reached out and plucked a bottle of shocking pink polish from the pyramid of shiny bottles. "New brand?"

Evangeline frowned. "Some rep came in earlier today. He works for Praxle's Potions."

"Praxle's? As in—"

"Yeah." Evangeline considered the stack of polishes. "They're working to rebuild their brand after the recent ... tarnishes. They want me to consider an endorsement deal."

My jaw dropped. "I hope you told them just what they could do with their offer!"

Evangeline sighed. "I told them I'd think about it."

"Oh, Evangeline." I shook my head. "You are way too nice."

"The stuff is total garbage," Lucy added with a grumpy

look at the bottle in my hands. "I could get the same result by dumping half a bottle of polish remover into any one of our existing lines of polish."

I wrinkled my nose and set the bottle down. The packaging was eye-catching and I was starting to see what the fuss was about. But surely people would give it a try once and then toss it when they realized how bad it was, right? How were they managing to *stay* in business?

"It's a sad day when scammers like Praxle are allowed to sell their potions free and clear while I'm banned from even *making* them anymore."

Evangeline and Lucy agreed with sympathetic looks.

The chime on the front of the shop chirped out a jingly little song and Ben sauntered into the shop. He took long, easy strides across the spa, heading for the back room where he had a massage studio, and flashed the three of us a wide grin. "How's it going, ladies?"

His voice, which I normally found appealing, sounded like nails on a chalkboard. I bristled and hurried to turn back to face Evangeline before my expression could give away my irritation.

"Doing just fine. Your three o'clock is ready for you," Lucy replied, her voice tart.

Ben nodded, seemingly oblivious to her venom, and passed through the emerald-green curtain that separated the retail and salon space from the treatment rooms in the back where massages, facials, and waxing services were provided.

"Mind if I use your bathroom before I go?" I asked Evangeline, already making my way to the curtain before she could reply.

I pushed through the thick fabric and nearly ran into Ben. "Oops!" He jumped back. "Sorry, Holly."

"No problem," I replied with a friendly smile. "Hey, I think I saw you in the haven today."

His face went white.

Busted!

"Actually, you were in the SPA building while I was on my way out. How do you know Sasha Pringle?"

He took another step back. "Who?"

I arched an eyebrow. Really? That's how he was going to play it?

His eyes darted to the door of his treatment room. "Sorry, Holly, I'd love to talk but I have someone waiting for me. We'll catch up later, okay?"

Before I could object, he yanked the door open and slinked into the room, closing the door soundly behind him.

CHAPTER 17

Using the excuse that my carton of ice cream was melting, I heaved my bags out the door of the day spa and hurried back to the manor. My head was swimming with new theories I wanted to run by Adam. When I reached the manor's front porch—cursing the heavy bags a little more with each step—my phone started to ring. "Oh, bat wings." I rolled my eyes, stashed the grocery bags on the top step, and retrieved my phone from the side pocket of my cross-body purse. "Hello?"

It was Harriet. "Hello Holly. Is this a good time?"

"Um, sure. What's up?"

"I wanted to let you know that there's been a development in Harvey's case. An arrest, actually."

I turned and plopped down on the steps beside the grocery bags. "Really?"

"They've arrested Dune Kasey. Agent Mache is the lead on the investigation and he's keeping everything pretty close to the vest. However, I did a little poking around, and from what I can tell, it looks like he used the Magic Beans portal right after Harvey."

"Whoa."

Talk about timing.

"They brought him in for questioning and he went ballistic, railing about the last time they put him away. Things must have escalated quite a bit because an hour later, he was arrested. I think they're still waiting to bring formal charges, but I wouldn't be surprised if this ends up on the news tonight. I didn't want you to be surprised, especially since we just spoke about him this afternoon."

I nodded, taking it all in. With Harvey being so high profile within the SPA, there hadn't been a doubt the agency would throw all of their available resources into finding his killer, but the swiftness of it still surprised me. "Thank you, Harriet. I really appreciate you letting me know."

"Of course. I know we both want the same thing. Justice for Harvey."

"Sounds like we're one step closer."

"Absolutely. I'll let you know if I hear anything else." She paused. "Oh, and Holly, it would be best if you keep this between us. I'm technically not supposed to share things like this. I'm sure you understand."

"Completely. Don't worry, Harriet. Thanks again for keeping me in mind."

We hung up and I sat on the porch for a long while, shuffling through everything one more time before going inside. Adam was still upstairs working, so after I put away the groceries I went to my room, got on my stomach, and fished the copy of the Haven Herald out from under the bed where Adam had recommended I keep it. Posy claimed she never visited our rooms, but if I were a ghost and had a bunch of interesting tenants, it was exactly what I would do. She could deny it all she wanted, but Posy was just as curious as anyone.

I sat on the floor with my back pressed up against the side

of the bed and unfolded the front page. Boots jumped down from the bed, landing with a loud thump as his paws hit the wood floor. He wandered over to inspect what I was doing but quickly lost interest when he realized it didn't involve food.

"Sorry, Bootsie," I said, scratching his head. He purred and curled up into a ball beside me.

The front page article of the paper detailed the Praxle case. The image still gave me the creeps and I tried to avoid looking at Praxle's arrogant expression as I read the words around it:

Bill Praxle is currently embroiled in a high-profile council proceeding that has captured the attention of the entire haven system. If convicted, he will likely face a life sentence. A number of heinous crimes are listed in the charges against him, including but not limited to: harassment, assault, extortion, embezzlement, and perjury.

"Charming man." I shook my head and then continued reading.

For more on this breaking story, tune into The Witch Wire tonight at 5 p.m. for a statement from Praxle's lawyer.

"Don't mind if I do," I said to myself. I had an hour to kill before the first broadcast of the news would start, so I went back to the kitchen and threw together a quick dinner, making sure there was enough for Adam whenever he was able to break away from work. I took my own bowl to the living room and flicked on the TV.

The Praxle case got the lion's share of the coverage and was much the same as the article I'd just finished reading. Despite the article's promise, there didn't appear to be any changes in the course of the day, even though the council hearing had gone on for eight hours.

Frustrated, I raised a hand, ready to flick the TV off, when the anchor's voice interrupted the tail-end of the story with a breaking update. I sat forward and listened intently.

"And in our top story of the night, the SPA has issued a public decree announcing that Vincent Mache has been appointed to the position of Grand Investigator here in the Seattle office. Following Harvey Colepepper's untimely death, the agency has kept quiet about plans to fill his position within the organization. However, an arrest was made earlier today in connection to that investigation. The details have not been publicly released, but it certainly appears the agency is confident in this development and is eager to move forward.

Mr. Mache has been a well-respected agent for nearly twelve years. He worked closely with Mr. Colepepper in his tenure at the agency and was, in fact, a former classmate of Mr. Colepepper's at academy.

It is noteworthy that Mr. Mache, while close to Mr. Colepepper, is at the opposite end of the spectrum on several hot-button issues presently facing haven society. One example that will likely garner attention in the coming days is his stance on technological development and forward movement. While the SPA and the Haven Council have long ruled against integrating technology—particularly the internet—within haven society, Mr. Mache is in favor of merging the tech world with that of magic and supernatural abilities. It is not clear how these ideals will play out, but one thing is for certain: expect some shake-ups.

Mr. Mache was unavailable for comment but we will be back, after the break, with a word from an SPA spokesperson."

The news transitioned to a commercial and I stared off into space, not fully seeing the flashy images showcasing some kind of enchanted hostess serving set that, according to the announcer, made fancy dinner parties a literal snap. My mind whirred back like a rewinding tape to the conversation with Adam after lunch. He'd mentioned one of the companies he worked for had been contacted by someone within the haven to see about bringing the supernatural world online and finally bridging that technological gap between humans and supers. According to the news report, that was something Agent Mache would be in agreement with, but that Harvey would have rejected. So, how was it that the order had already been placed? Harvey had outranked Mache, so he would have been the one to vote in new orders.

I pushed off the floor and went upstairs to Adam's room. I knocked twice, lightly, and he told me to come in. Adam was hunched over his desk, his eyes bouncing between two huge monitors. "Hey, Holls. I swear I'm almost done here."

I perched on the edge of his bed. "Sorry to interrupt, but I wanted to ask you something."

"Shoot," he said without looking away from his work. His fingers flew over the keys, typing so fast it was almost startling.

"You said something about the haven wanting to get some kind of supers-specific internet base set up."

"Uh, yeah." *Click, click, click-click-click.* "They contracted Stars Burst Enterprises to set up a preliminary database for some big meeting coming up."

"Stars Burst?"

Adam laughed. "I know, it always gets me thinking about candy."

I rolled my eyes. "What doesn't?"

He craned around and gave me a playful scowl. "Why are you asking about it? I probably shouldn't have even mentioned it. They're keeping it under wraps, I assume because they don't want to start a public debate until it's officially happening."

"Agent Mache has been named as Harvey's replacement," I said, still putting the other pieces together in the back of my mind. "It was on *The Witch Wire* tonight."

Adam's eyebrows lifted. "Wow. That was fast."

"And they arrested Dune Kasey," I added.

Adam looked down at the large face of his watch. "How long have I been up here?"

"Harriet called me. That part, the arrest, just happened this afternoon."

"And they waited what, a whole two hours to name Mache as the new Grand Investigator?"

"Yeah. I don't like it. It feels too rushed."

Adam slung an arm over the back of his chair and spun to face me. "What are you thinking?"

"I don't know yet," I said with a small shake of my head. "But it doesn't sit right."

"I suppose the SPA needs to move on but it does seem kind of *bam, bam, bam.*"

"Here's what I'm wondering: if Agent Mache was in charge of the murder investigation, which is what Harriet said and Agent Bramble implied, then would he be motivated to find the truth, or was he just trying to close the case so he could get on with his promotion? I mean, when I was with Agent Bramble she seemed a little annoyed with Agent Mache. There was that whole campaigning comment that sounded a little bitter. Harriet already told me some of his comments were rubbing people the wrong way. Why should we trust the results of his investigation if his real motive is to get a job promotion?"

"Sounds like you need to talk to Agent Bramble if you want to dig into this," Adam said. "She was his partner. If anyone knows what's going on, it'll be her."

I gave a half-cocked smile. "Do I need to brace myself for the part where you tell me I should stay out of it because I don't need to get tangled up in another investigation, and that it will all work itself out?"

Adam returned my grin. "I've learned that you're gonna

do what you want regardless. It's easier if I just step back and prepare to be your muscle if needed."

I got up from the bed and sat in his lap, looping my arms around his neck. "You're a very smart man, St. James. Have I mentioned that lately?"

He chuckled and put one hand behind my neck. He guided my lips to his and kissed me softly.

I pulled back and smiled at him. "Now, how about you turn off all these contraptions so we can get to our date?"

He ran a thumb over my cheek and gave me one more kiss. "Yes ma'am."

∽

I DOZED through the end of the movie and woke up long enough to say goodnight to Adam before we padded off to our respective rooms. I'd been exhausted after dinner, but when I climbed into bed beside Boots, my mind kicked back into high gear and rambled through the different theories and worries all over again. I rolled over and buried my face in the pillow, wishing I could muffle the musings of my distracted mind.

It was pointless.

With an irritated sigh, I threw off the blankets and stuffed my feet into my slippers. I made my way to the kitchen, surprised to find Lacey and Posy already there. That was an unusual late-night pairing. They said hello as I wandered in and put on the kettle, intending to dose myself with some sleep-inducing tea to quiet my thoughts.

"I haven't seen you in a while, Lacey. Everything okay?"

"Just fine," she said before taking a long sip from her crystal goblet of faux blood. "You? Any progress with Nick?"

"Ugh." I leaned against the counter and shook my head. "None at all. I stopped at a potion shop in the haven a couple days ago, but that was a total bust. The only thing the potions master had was something that would need to be administered each day. I don't even *see* Nick every day, so unless I turn into a total stalker, that's not really going to work."

"Adam probably loves that idea," Lacey quipped with a grin.

"Did the potions master have any other suggestions, dear?" Posy asked.

The kettle boiled and I paused to mix up a large cup of tea. "He told me to find someone skilled at mind magic, which is not helpful in the slightest." I carried my tea to the table and sat down. "For starters, I'm really not sure where to even *look* for someone like that. After all, it's not exactly the kind of thing people advertise on billboards."

"Isn't it illegal?" Posy asked.

"Technically yes, since it involves a human. I might have left that part out when talking to the potions master."

"The potions master didn't have any names for you?" Lacey asked.

I shook my head. "No. Or at least none that he offered up."

"See, this is why I avoid the haven," Lacey said defiantly. "The whole thing is so complicated!"

"And vampire life isn't?" I countered with a pointed look. "I think after that whole mess with Raven and the so-called Vampire Council, I'll take my chances with the haven."

Lacey shrugged. "Suit yourself. To me, the afterlife is complicated enough; why make it harder with all these rules and regulations?"

"You're not saying you agree with the Vampire Council are you?" Posy asked, trying—and failing—to hide the disgust on her face.

"I'd rather not be a part of either, but at least with the Vampire Council, things are more cut and dried. If I want to change someone's mind about something, I can glamour them. Now, if I did that inside the haven, they'd flip out and have me arrested!"

Glamour? I sat up straighter. "Lacey, could you glamour Nick into forgetting about the night of the raid?"

Posy's silvery eyebrows hiked up her forehead as her eyes whipped toward me. "Holly!"

"I'm sorry, Posy, but I'm getting desperate. Nick needs to forget the events of that night and I'm afraid that if I report it to the SPA, they'll take him and lock him up for some kind of testing to see why the original spell didn't work. Or they'll just obliterate his entire memory to be safe. I can't allow that."

Posy huffed. "Well I'm not going to be a part of this!" With that, she surged up toward the ceiling, as fast as I'd ever seen her move, and vanished.

"And somehow I get labeled as the dramatic one? At least I don't shake the house off its foundation when I'm having a bad day." Lacey rolled her eyes. "As to your question, yes, I could glamour him and pluck out those memories, but it would have to be soon. After a certain amount of time passes, it becomes harder to isolate certain memories and I'd be no better than some SPA goon with a wand."

She hopped down from the counter, rinsed her crystal goblet in the sink, and returned it to its cabinet by the fridge. Before leaving the kitchen, she stopped at the door, tossed her long platinum hair over her shoulder, and shrugged. "Let me know, okay?"

I nodded. "I will. Thanks, Lacey."

She pursed her lips and pushed out of the kitchen.

CHAPTER 18

The next morning, I took the portal into the haven with Evangeline at my side. Adam was still swamped with work, so Evangeline offered to tag along and keep me company. As we walked through the haven streets, I filled her in on the strange late-night conversation with Lacey and Posy.

"I don't know if glamouring is the best solution," she finally said.

"Why not?"

Evangeline glanced over at me. "Well it's illegal for a reason, right? I mean there must be some type of danger or risks associated with it."

"Honestly, I don't know anymore. After all the hubbub with the Vampire Council vs the Haven Council, it seems like the Haven Council might make it illegal simply because they don't want the vamps to have any kind of edge."

Evangeline frowned. "That's very political of you."

I shrugged. "When I used to live in the haven, I never really saw it, you know? Now that I've lived outside of the haven for a year and met so many different kinds of people, supers and humans alike, it's really opened my eyes to the way the haven works. They say they're inclusive, but just last night on *The Witch Wire*, they were talking about the controversy surrounding the appointment of a shifter to the Grand Investigator position and whether or not it's a good idea to have non-magic wielders in such positions of power. And as for vamps, I don't think a single one works for the SPA."

"I'm not saying you're wrong, Holly. Maybe it's perfectly safe and even best in situations like this. I'd just say to be very careful. You're already in a precarious position with the council."

"Don't I know it," I sighed. "I can't tell you how much I miss potion work. I've started dreaming about it. The plants in the greenhouse are all starting to go crazy as spring gets closer, and I can't stop myself from thinking about all the things I want to create and make."

"I'm sure Teddy will figure something out," she said cheerfully.

I wasn't so sure.

I told her about Sasha and the tiny bit of information I was able to extract from Adam's internet search. Then, after hesitating for a moment, I told her about Ben.

"Ben? Why would he be at the SPA headquarters?"

I held up my hands. "I don't know. They looked … friendly with one another. But when I asked him about her, he acted like he had no idea who I was talking about. It was weird."

Evangeline's eyebrows lifted. It was well known around town that Ben and Evangeline were flirty with one another. Evangeline had resisted his attempts to ask her out on a date, citing that it would be inappropriate since she was technically his boss, but that hadn't seemed to slow either one of them down when it came to longing looks, coy smiles, and shared inside jokes. Then again, that was all before Teddy had come back into her daily life. Maybe her feelings toward Ben had changed.

"I don't really care who he spends time with, obviously," Evangeline said, her brows still arched. "But the fact that he's leaving work and taking time off to do it, and then lying about it, is clearly not acceptable."

I nodded. "Although, I suppose it's possible he *was* at the doctor's and stopped by to have lunch with a friend afterward."

"Yes, but he was late getting back," Evangeline quickly pointed out. "He had a client waiting for him. If he was out having some kind of social engagement, he should have scheduled it for a time when he wasn't expected back at work."

"Agreed."

"The better question is what he's doing palling around with someone like her. From what you and Teddy told me, she sounds absolutely awful!"

I frowned. "Understatement."

"Ben's such a nice guy. Warm and friendly. He doesn't even act like a werewolf." She stopped and shot me a guilty look. "Not that I'm saying—"

"Don't worry, Evangeline." I smiled at her flustered expression. "I know what you mean. He's very social for a were."

Werewolves were usually the hermit type. Not many of them chose to live within the haven system, and found themselves more at home within the human world where it was easier to blend in.

"None of it makes sense," Evangeline concluded with a shake of her head. "Do you want me to try to ask him about it? Or about her?"

"No. I don't think that's a good idea. Teddy is working the legal channels to find a way to get me a fair hearing. Meanwhile, Adam is working with some of his dad's law enforcement contacts to see what he can find out about Ms. Pringle."

Evangeline's almond-shaped eyes gleamed. "Oh! That's good!"

We rounded the corner onto the main street through the haven. We stopped a few paces down the sidewalk and gawked at the huge crowd clogging the street in front of a shop. We paused and looked at the source of the commotion: a Pepto-Bismol-pink building with a huge glittering marque sign hanging above it. Every few seconds, the sign shot off pink and white fireworks.

"Praxle's Potions." I sneered up at the sign before dropping my gaze to the line of people waiting to get inside for the grand opening door-busters offered on splashy signs that had been distributed all throughout the haven. "It's like the council hearing isn't even happening. Why are they all supporting this ... this *gangster*?"

Lines etched Evangeline's face as it twisted into a glower. "I have half a mind to go in there and tell them—loudly—just what I think about their nail polish!"

"Not sure your opinion was quite the endorsement deal they were hoping for," I said with a laugh. "Although if you're serious, let's stop at the corner store so I can grab some popcorn beforehand."

The visual image of Evangeline storming into the store, fists on her hips and screaming about watered down nail polish, made me smile. She was one of the most mild-mannered witches I'd ever met and was extremely humble, regardless of her status as the former star of a very popular paranormal soap opera.

For a second, I thought she was actually going to lunge forward and burst through the line of people at the door but after a moment, she scoffed at the shop and the crowd, and then grabbed my elbow and propelled me down the walk.

"Let's get out of here. I don't want anyone to think I'm here for some kind of signing event."

We pushed into the SPA building and I made my way to the reception desk. Though I didn't have an appointment, I told the receptionist I needed to speak with Agent Bramble. The brassy woman eyed me warily but picked up her phone and dialed her extension. The two exchanged a few words and then the receptionist set the phone down and folded her hands politely. "It could be a while. Agent Bramble is *very* busy. Are you sure you want to wait? I could send up a message if you'd prefer." Her voice was sticky sweet and made Agent Bramble's message crystal clear: get rid of her!

I returned the smarmy grin and mirrored her tone as I informed her that I would wait as long as it took. The receptionist pointed me to a group of chairs and then picked up the phone again. She was muttering to Agent Bramble as soon as Evangeline and I turned away.

"I swear, my missing-personality-chip theory gets stronger every time I come here," I told Evangeline as we sat down.

~

IT WAS NEARLY an hour later when Agent Bramble finally realized I was just stubborn enough to wait all day if that's what it took and called me up to her office. Evangeline wished me luck and then headed out to get some shopping done while I was in the meeting. Before she left, we agreed to meet by the fountain in front of the large Haven Bank building one street over from the headquarters building.

"Hello Holly," Agent Bramble said, barely hiding a cringe when she ushered me into her cramped office. It was just as neat as it was during my last visit. However, this time the shades between her office and Agent Mache's former office were drawn. I wondered if he'd already taken over Harvey's elegant office. I hoped if he had, he'd show it more respect than he had his previous space.

"I do apologize for the wait," Agent Bramble continued after taking her seat. "Things have been understandably busy around here with all the changes. I don't mean to be brisk with you, but what is this *unscheduled* visit about?"

I crossed one leg over the other. "Agent Bramble, I know you don't know me. But I need you to trust me and listen to what I have to say. Despite what looks like a tumultuous relationship on paper, I respected Harvey, and in the weeks before his death we were finally starting to see eye to eye. It is very important to me that the person who killed him is dealt with."

Agent Bramble's expression lightened. "Then you'll be relieved to hear we currently have someone in custody with ties to the murder. We're waiting on some tests to come back, but it looks like we have our man."

"You're talking about Dune Kasey?"

Her thin eyebrows shot up. "How do you know his name?" Her hand whipped toward her phone. "Was it in the paper this morning? I haven't had a chance to look. Those good-for-nothing vultures—"

"No!" I hurried to say. "No, it wasn't in the papers."

She kept her hand on the phone. "Then where did you get that name?"

"I reviewed some of Harvey's old cases. I know Dune was recently released from prison and that he's made some ... outlandish claims to the papers. But I don't think he's the one who killed Harvey."

She raised her eyebrows. "You don't?"

"No."

Agent Bramble sighed and released her grip on the phone.

"And do you have any evidence or proof to back up this theory?"

"It's simple," I said. "What reason did he have for killing Harvey? Sure, he might be angry that Harvey was part of the sting operation that sent him to prison. But how likely is it that less than a month after his release, he would go after Harvey in such an obvious way? He'd have to know the fingers would point his way, especially with the way he's spouted off to the Herald. I've read the articles. He's clearly not a good person, but I don't think that's good enough evidence."

"Ms. Boldt—"

"It also doesn't make sense that Harvey would let him into his car. If someone publicly threatened me, I certainly wouldn't agree to meet with them—especially alone—and then drink a cup of coffee they purchased for me! It doesn't make any sense! Harvey was many things, but stupid wasn't one of them."

Agent Bramble rubbed her temples, then reached up and adjusted her glasses. "Mr. Kasey was unable to provide a reasonable alibi to the agents who interviewed him. What we know is that he used the portal at the Magic Beans coffee shop to pass from the haven into Seattle proper mere minutes after Harvey did."

"So what is the working theory? He ordered a coffee after Harvey and dumped some potion into it while he wasn't looking?"

Agent Bramble didn't justify my objection with a response. "We're not in a position to discuss the evidence until the trial is in motion. I've already said too much. You're not in law enforcement, Holly. You don't have privileges here. You need to step back and trust the SPA to handle this case."

I uncrossed my legs and dropped my foot to the floor

with a louder-than-intended *stomp*. Agent Bramble bristled. "Maybe I could trust the SPA to conduct a thorough investigation, but the fact is that it's currently being run by someone who is probably more concerned with picking out window treatments and furniture for his new office!" The words flew from my mouth faster than I could think to reign them in.

Agent Bramble lifted a hand, her palm facing me in a clear signal. "Stop! Ms. Boldt, that is quite enough. You cannot simply waltz in here and question the integrity of the entire SPA!"

"I'm not! Simply the man they've just put at the top of the crime division."

"What does Agent Mache even have to do with your theory?"

I considered her for a moment, briefly wondering what she might do to me if I said what I really thought. Would she throw me out of her office? Ban me from the SPA building in general? Arrest me?

I shoved aside the risk. "Who benefits the most from Harvey's death? Seems to me Agent Mache is pretty close to the top of the list. Now, I'm not a detective, but I have inadvertently stumbled into a few investigations over the past year and I know a detective or private eye starts an investigation by looking for a motive. Who wanted Harvey dead? Could it be a revenge killing? Maybe. But it makes more sense that someone wanted him out of the way because they'd benefit from it."

"This is outrageous!"

"Ask Mache about his plans for the internet!" I spewed before she could throw me out on my backside.

Her sharp eagle-eyes snapped to me. "What did you say?"

Adam was going to kill me.

CHAPTER 19

"Well, how did it go?" Evangeline asked. She was sitting on the edge of the fountain picking apart a scone while she waited for me.

I plopped down beside her and frowned. "Not great. But hey, I'm still alive and not in jail, so obviously it could have gone worse."

"I'm sorry."

"She told me I'm way off base, but is giving me a pass because of everything I've been through."

"It will all come out in the end, Holly. These things usually can't stay buried for long. Have you considered floating the theory about Mache to a reporter? Teddy knows a few of the Herald writers down in LA. He could probably make some calls and get you in touch with someone."

I weighed the idea. It wasn't bad, but it could also trigger some tricky after-effects. "I'll think about it. Maybe if they could keep my name out of the whole thing. I don't know if I can afford to make any more enemies. As it is, I want to march upstairs and find Sasha Pringle's office and demand to know what her problem is!"

Evangeline smiled. "Probably not the best call but if you need backup, I'm your girl."

"Thanks." I motioned toward the bags at Evangeline's feet. "Looks like your time was better spent."

She laughed, the sound soft and melodic. "I picked up a few things."

To Evangeline, *a few things* was the equivalent of an all-expense-paid shopping spree for most people. I guess she had to do *something* with all her leftover soap star cash.

"Actually, there was an interesting development, besides the killer sale at Voro's shoe store. I ran into Bill Praxle on my way here."

"What? Where?" I looked around, as if expecting him to materialize right in front of me.

"He was sneaking out the back of that new shop we passed on our way to the SPA building." She finished her scone and wiped her sticky fingers off on a teal napkin from the bakery around the corner. "I was surprised to see him. I guess I figured the SPA had him in custody."

I shook my head. "No, he's a free man till the council hearing is over."

"Well I wasn't trying to get his attention, but he spotted me and wanted to chat about the possibility of my endorsement deal."

I laughed. "Seriously?"

"It was really weird, Holly. It's like he doesn't even realize he's been on trial for the last week and a half. Completely unfazed."

"What did you tell him?"

She gave a mischievous grin. "That I'd meet him for an early dinner."

"What?" I hissed.

She laughed and waved an unconcerned hand at my shocked expression. "I have a plan."

"I sure hope so!"

"I want you to go with me. You can ask him about Harvey and see what he says."

I scoffed. "He's not going to tell me anything." I paused, my mouth still open. "Unless …"

Without another word I tore into my purse. My fingers clawed through the mess of contents: lipsticks—way too many lipsticks—a compact mirror, a spare pair of stockings, a bag of chocolates, half a Lemon Cloud wrapped in wax paper, and an assortment of potion vials. When I reached the vials, I started pulling them out one by one. When I found the one I was searching for, my lips curved up into a smile that matched Evangeline's.

I twisted the vial around so she could see the label. "Unless he gets a sip of this."

"Good ole Loose Lips."

～

IT WAS INSANE, but I was counting on the old adage "crazy enough that it just might work" to get us by. Evangeline and I wandered the shops for a couple of hours to kill time and perfect our plan. Finally, we made our way back to the center of the haven and arrived at Luna, a popular—and very expensive—restaurant that Praxle had chosen for the meeting.

I'd never been inside Luna before and as soon as we stepped inside, I had to stop and gawk at the beautiful restaurant. It seemed impossible that there was a bustling street with noise and traffic and chaos just on the other side of the large wooden doors. The atmosphere was clearly a literal interpretation of the restaurant's name. It was like being wrapped in a blanket made of stars. The walls were dark—an inky midnight blue—lit with the soft glow of what seemed like thousands of candles floating in midair along the walls and ceiling. The burnished mahogany furniture contrasted with the crisp white linens and soft accents of gold and pearl.

It was pure magic within a city teeming with it.

A hostess wearing a sleek black cocktail dress with stars splashed across it guided us up a wrought-iron spiral staircase to a private dining area. There were several tables scattered around the room, most set for two, but only one was occupied.

"Hello, Mr. Praxle," Evangeline said, floating across the room to where Bill Praxle was seated. He stood, buttoned his suit jacket, and greeted her with a friendly embrace.

"This is Holly Boldt, my friend I told you about."

"Ah, yes, the potion goddess," he said, his voice oil-slick.

Fitting. It matched his greased up hair.

"Goddess?" I cocked an eyebrow at Evangeline.

She laughed and waved a hand. "All I said was that you're the best potions witch I've ever met, and believe me, in LA they are a dime a dozen and always trying to peddle something!"

Praxle gestured to the two chairs at his table, inviting us to sit. Once we did, he took his own place and promptly ordered a bottle of wine. An *expensive* bottle of wine. I nearly choked when I saw the prices on the card that sat at my left elbow.

"Something you should know about me is that I want the best of everything," Praxle started once the wine was poured. "My shops are expanding rapidly in all of the major West Coast havens and I have an eye on the East Coast just as soon as I get past all of this ... red tape."

My eyebrows arched. Red tape? That's what he called being on trial for a laundry list of charges? A list where assault was actually one of the *lesser* crimes?

Evangeline didn't say anything but I caught a slight smile as she lifted her wine glass to take a sip.

Praxle drank deeply from his own glass and then set it aside. He folded his long, slender fingers together and then leaned forward on the table. "I'm working on something top-secret and I would *love* to get some kind of contract in place with a truly talented potions master. What do you say, Holly?"

"We just met," I said without thinking.

Praxle laughed. "I've been in this business a long time, Holly. I know talent when I see it and I'm very good at reading people."

I gave a slight nod. "Right."

"Now, Bill, there is one thing I forgot to mention," Evangeline interjected. His eyes swiveled to her. "Holly's having a little trouble with the council approving her potions master license. She wouldn't be able to do anything until that was cleared up."

Praxle waved a hand. "Ah, don't worry about the council."

I reached for my wine glass. "Sounds like an odd statement coming from someone who's in the center of one of the biggest council hearings of the past few years."

I expected Praxle to bristle at my not-so-gentle reminder of his current reality. Instead he smiled wider. "What can I say? I'm confident the entire *misunderstanding* will be resolved quickly and without further hindrance to my enterprises. Believe me, I wouldn't be asking the lovely Evangeline Loren to tarnish her bright star by associating with my company if I thought things were going to go south."

Evangeline gave a demure smile. I'd never realized before how cunning she could be. Praxle would never pick up on her true feelings about his business practices or inferior products. Hours ago, she'd stood in front of his newest shop, ready to tear it to pieces. Now she sat across from him with enthusiasm and charm as though they were long-time friends.

"Well I certainly am glad to hear that," she said, followed by a tinkling laugh. She raised her glass.

Praxle watched her, not bothering to conceal the desire in his eyes, before shifting his gaze back to me. "So, Holly, what types of potion work are you most comfortable with? More of a replicator? Or do you dabble with custom formulas?"

"Custom potions are my specialty. As a private vendor, I'm able to work closely with my clients to create something special and unique to meet their needs."

Bill nodded. "Any experience with mass production? I don't mind having a line of exclusive, limited-edition products, but my bread and butter is in the wham-bam, assembly-line stuff."

I disguised a grimace with a polite smile. Potions weren't *stuff* and they certainly weren't produced on an assembly line. If that was his mentality, it made sense why the enchanted nail polish he'd had delivered to The Emerald was so inferior to even non-magic products. Had no one explained these basic business principles to him? Or had people tried and he simply ignored them?

"I'm sure we could arrange something," I said, burying all the arguments racing through my mind. "Tell you what—would you like to try a sample of my work?" I asked sweetly, producing the now-unmarked vial from my purse. "This is a custom creation."

Praxle took the vial and held it up to one of the soft lights hovering above the table. He twisted the cylinder slowly, watching the contents intently. "What does it do?"

"It's a memory boost. Do you ever have that feeling like you're forgetting something? Like when you're packing for a trip?"

"That happens to me all the time!" Evangeline chimed in.

Praxle didn't look convinced. "I have assistants for packing."

"Right."

Evangeline swooped in to the rescue. "What about the feeling when you go to get something, say from the office, only to get there and realize you've completely forgotten what you needed?"

"Ah!" Praxle's eyes widened. "Yes, now that is a real problem."

"Great!" I flicked a grateful smile at Evangeline. "Well this potion will instantly bring to top of mind whatever it was you forgot. Saving time and, of course, aggravation."

"All right," Praxle said. He popped the cork from the small vial. "How should I test it?"

"Take the potion and then we'll ask you to recall something. You'll see how fast you can produce the answer."

He nodded and then dropped his head back. He swallowed the swig of potion and then corked the empty vial and handed it to me. "You need new packaging," he said. "This isn't going to win any kind of award."

Right, that was my concern.

Praxle washed down the potion with another sip of wine and then refolded his hands. He looked expectantly from me to Evangeline. "All right, ask away."

Don't mind if I do ...

"Why don't you tell me about Harvey Colepepper," I prompted.

Praxle's thick eyebrows scrunched together. "Harvey Colepepper? The vindictive little SPA troll?"

"Goblin-hybrid," I said. "He's the one who arrested you, isn't that right?"

Praxle's face twisted into a bitter expression. "Yes."

"Is the reason you're not worried about the council

hearing because Harvey is gone and now your friend Mache is at the top of the SPA? You think he'll get you off?"

Praxle gave a wide, menacing grin. "Mache isn't going to let me go to prison. He's biding his time but he'll get these ridiculous, baseless charges thrown out!"

I narrowed my eyes. I'd only used the potion on one other occasion, and it was on a human. I had no idea how long it would last on a shifter who knew he'd taken something mind-altering. It was time to go in for the kill. "Did you hire one of your flunkies to poison Harvey Colepepper?"

"No!" Praxle pushed back from the table.

"Did Mache have it arranged?"

Praxle started shaking his head violently. "I don't think this potion is working."

I flashed a cold smile. "Oh, trust me, it's working just fine."

"Security!" Praxle shouted.

Two large men moved from the shadows and lumbered over to stand behind Praxle.

"What did you give me?"

"Something to help you tell the truth, for once in your sorry life," I snapped.

He pointed at me and then turned his glower on Evangeline. "Get out of here and never cross my path again or I'll have both of you thrown in jail!"

I rolled my eyes. "Oh yeah? You putting an ad out for roommates?"

Praxle sneered. Evangeline grabbed my arm and hustled me from the table. We rushed down the spiral stairs and out the front door without stopping long enough to look back to see if the two huge bodyguards were on our tail.

CHAPTER 20

With our heels firmly planted back on square one, Evangeline and I headed back to Beechwood Harbor. On the way back to the manor, Evangeline announced that she needed to stop in at The Emerald and check in. I offered to go with her. I felt aimless. Defeated. I hadn't been able to help solve Harvey's case, I still had no idea what to do to get my potions license, Nick was still running around thinking he was halfway out of his mind, and my temporary SPA case worker thought I was a total basket case.

The Emerald was technically closed for the night, had been for about half an hour, but the lights were still on and two figures stood inside, visible from the street. One of them was Lucy and the other was a woman I didn't recognize. Neither of them looked happy.

Evangeline's brow furrowed and she quickened her pace, pushing into the salon moments before me. Loud voices greeted us as we stepped inside. The woman opposite Lucy towered over her petite frame. Her dark hair was pulled back in a low ponytail and she appeared to be in her mid-forties.

"—supposed to be a vacation and instead of having a relaxing afternoon, I wasted over an hour waiting for my masseuse to come back into the room! I've had a lot of massages and never have I felt so completely humiliated and mistreated!" Her fists dug into her hips as she leaned closer and closer to Lucy with each word.

I hung back near the door, but Evangeline charged forward, taking her place beside Lucy. "Excuse me!" she snapped in an authoritative tone I'd never heard her use before. "Can I interrupt here and ask that you not shout at my employee?"

The tall woman's eyes snapped to Evangeline and her lips twisted into a scowl. "You're the owner of this dump?"

I winced.

Evangeline visibly drew in a breath. "I am the owner of this salon. May I ask for your name?" she said coolly.

"Tara Doyle. I had a four o'clock appointment with your masseuse, Ben something-or-other. He didn't even bother to introduce himself properly!"

Evangeline looked at Lucy out of the corner of her eye. Lucy was paler than usual and I wondered how long Ms. Doyle had been berating her before we'd shown up.

Lucy nodded and the woman proceeded. "Less than ten minutes into the massage, his phone rang. His ringtone sounded three or four times, which was extremely distracting. I made the comment that maybe he should answer it, thinking he would take the hint and silence the stupid thing. Instead, he actually had the nerve to take the call!"

Evangeline's full lips went razor thin. She prided herself on running a prestigious day spa even though Beechwood Harbor was a casual town. Apart from the tourist season in the summer, there wasn't a lot of action but that didn't matter to Evangeline. She ran the place as though it were smack-dab in the middle of Rodeo Drive. Top-of-the-line products, exceptional service, and accommodations for clients with special requests. To her, Ben's actions weren't just unprofessional, but an all-out assault on her establishment.

"He stepped out after a few minutes, leaving me stranded and half nude on the table. It took twenty minutes before I realized he wasn't coming back! I got dressed and came out here, where this woman assured me that she could get Ben back to complete the massage and that there would be no charge. For some reason that is now beyond me, I waited around, in a robe, for another hour! I left and got all the way back to my hotel before I decided to come back and let you know this is unacceptable treatment! I will be leaving you negative reviews on as many websites as I can find! Your business might as well close up shop now."

"Okay, hold on," Evangeline said, holding up one hand. "First of all, let me offer my most sincere apology. I have no idea why Ben would have acted in such an unprofessional manner, and I can assure you he will be dealt with. He's never had complaints or a negative review during his entire time here, so this is shocking but I agree it's completely unacceptable. As for your time, there's obviously no way I can give that back to you, but please, let me attempt to make it up to you. Where are you staying? I'll have a basket of complimentary products sent to you, as well as a gift certificate to the best restaurant in town."

The woman bristled. She'd clearly been amped for another fight, which Evangeline immediately dissolved with her warm tone and generous offer. "I—I'm staying at the Sea Castle."

"Wonderful!" Evangeline clasped her hands together. "I know right where that is and I will personally deliver the basket to the front desk by tomorrow afternoon. Will that work? You'll still be in town?"

The woman nodded and reached up to tuck away a strand of hair that had escaped her ponytail. "I'll be here through the weekend."

"Okay. I am truly sorry, Ms. Doyle, and I hope this hasn't ruined your stay here in our little town."

"I'm not happy about the lost time, but I accept your apology." Ms. Doyle gave a curt nod, pivoted on the heel of her designer shoes, and made her way to the door. I held it open for her and she muttered her thanks, then stalked down the sidewalk.

"Bat wings," I said when I stepped back inside. "That was Herculean self-control, Evangeline. I think I would have jinxed her or something."

Evangeline attempted a smile but it didn't warm her dark eyes. "If I'm going to jinx anyone, it's Ben!" She rounded on Lucy who had moved back to the reception desk. "Where did he go? Did he say anything?"

Lucy shook her head. "I have no idea. I was in the middle of a manicure when he just ... left. He didn't look happy. I had no idea he'd walked out on his client until she came storming out. I tried his cell phone at least a dozen times. The first few times it rang through to his voicemail but the last few it just cut off, like he'd either shut off the phone or was rejecting my calls."

Evangeline's hands clenched into tight fists as she stood in one place. "I'll find him. In the meantime, can you print off all the resumes we're received from massage therapists over the past few months? I'm officially opening a position."

~

Evangeline walked at such a clip back to the manor that I nearly had to jog to keep up with her. She muttered and fumed with each step and when we burst through the front door, Adam stopped mid-stride and looked at us. "Evening, ladies?" he said cautiously.

"You're a hacker, right?" Evangeline boomed in reply.

Adam turned and stared at her. "No. Why? You in the market?"

"No!" She snapped, throwing her hands in the air. "I was just making conversation!"

Adam and I exchanged shocked looks and I put an arm over Evangeline's shoulders. "We're on your side here."

"What happened?" Adam asked.

I filled him in.

"Well, I can't hack his phone," Adam said when I finished. "Sorry. What's plan B?"

Evangeline set her shopping bags onto the floor and then started digging in her purse. She pulled a keyring out and held it up. "Let's go pay Ben a visit."

"Are you sure, Evie?" Adam asked.

She looked at me. "It's what Nick would do, right? If he was trying to figure out what someone was up to?"

I shrugged. "I guess so, yeah."

"Well then that's what I want to do. Figure out what he's up to."

"Have you tried calling him?" Adam asked.

Evangeline scowled at him. "Of course!"

"Well, actually, *you* haven't tried," I pointed out. "Lucy did."

"I don't know what difference it will make," she grumbled, diving back into her purse. She retrieved her phone and smashed her finger against the screen a few times before raising the device to her ear. She glared at the wall as it rang through. Then her eyebrows lifted. "Ben?"

Adam and I exchanged a glance and moved to flank Evangeline. She pulled the phone away and tapped speakerphone. "Ben, it's Evangeline."

"Evie, I'm so sorry—" he started, his voice slightly muffled, as though he had his hand cupped around the phone to keep his voice from carrying. "I can explain everything."

"We're past explanations, Benjamin. This isn't working for me. I've worked too hard to make The Emerald the success that it is, and a huge part of that success comes from having a staff of dedicated professionals. I am saddened to say it, but your recent behavior doesn't meet those standards."

"No! Evangeline, please let me explain," he begged, his voice louder and tinged with urgency.

Evangeline paused, her head cocked as she stared down at the illuminated screen. "You have two minutes. Convince me."

Adam looked over at me, his eyebrows lifted.

"*I know*," I mouthed.

"As you know, I've been going to the doctor a lot lately. I've been having odd symptoms. I wanted to tell you about it, but I wasn't sure how …"

"What's going on?" Evangeline asked, some of the coldness leaving her tone.

"I'm starting to change, into a, well, you know, mid-cycle. Not a full change, but enough that I can't work sometimes."

My heart sank. How awful.

"Ben," Evangeline said, her eyes closed. "Why didn't you tell me sooner?"

"I didn't want to lose my job. But now it seems like that's already happened."

Evangeline shifted back and forth. "Well, I—"

"Who is that?" a second, female voice cut in.

Ben cursed.

"Who is that?" Evangeline asked.

"Uh—no one. Listen, I gotta—"

"Benjamin, I'm not kidding. I will have your mangy hide

turned into a throw rug if you don't get in here right now!" the female voice cut in, not an ounce of warmth or playfulness in her threat.

All three of us flinched.

Evangeline pulled the phone closer to her mouth. "Ben, what is going on? Are you in trouble?"

"Evie I'm—I'm sorry—"

The line went dead.

Evangeline stared at the phone for a moment then frantically redialed three more times, but each one went straight to voicemail. Distressed, she turned to us. "What do you think that was about?"

"I have no idea, but it didn't sound good," Adam replied.

Evangeline's green eyes shifted to me, searching for answers.

I started to shrug, then froze. "Wait a second. I know that voice."

"Who is it?"

My hands curled into fists. "Sasha Pringle."

CHAPTER 21

Adam turned to me. "Holly, are you sure?"

"Positive." The goosebumps on my arms were proof enough. Her mocking voice was ingrained in my mind; I'd have recognized it anywhere.

"What are we supposed to do now?" Evangeline asked. She dialed Ben's number again, but the call was blocked. "It sounds like he could be in serious trouble. We can't just sit here! We heard her threaten him."

"Slow down, Evie," Adam said, his tone even and soothing. "We don't know anything yet. For all we know, that was some kind of joke. Granted, a pretty sick one. Holly saw Sasha and Ben together at the SPA headquarters. She said they looked like friends ... or maybe more than friends."

"Yeah, but I don't know if I'm buying his doctor story. He didn't look sick or mid-change to me when I saw him with Sasha at the SPA building. The bigger question is how in the Otherworld do they even know each other?"

Evangeline looked to me. "Do you think he's lying about the change thing?"

"I don't know. I mean, he sounded pretty genuine about

it, but I've never heard of a were having issues changing mid-lunar cycle. That part doesn't make any sense."

"But *why* would he lie?" Evangeline pressed.

Adam shrugged. "To keep his job?"

She shook her head. "Maybe, but I can't let this go. We have to find a way to help him."

I chewed on the corner of my lip, searching for an idea.

Adam perked. "Wait one second. I may have something."

Without elaborating, he bolted up the stairs, taking them two at a time. Evangeline and I exchanged a puzzled look but neither one of us said anything. Adam bounded back down the stairs a moment later, a scrap of lined notebook paper in his hand. "I have Sasha's address."

"You do?" We said in unison.

"I was trying to track down more information about her. She lives in the haven."

"What were you planning to do? Spy on her?" I asked him.

He shrugged. "Hey, that's what Nick would do. Although, I'm pretty sure it's called *surveillance* in that case."

He had a point.

"You're right. That's far less creepy," I said.

Evangeline handed Adam her keys. "You drive!"

"Can't we take the portal?" Adam asked me.

I shook my head. "They aren't open when the SPA building is closed up for the night. It won't work."

With a grin, Adam held up Evangeline's keys and jingled them. "Then I guess we're road trippin'!"

Adam drove Evangeline's car all the way to Seattle. With his lead foot and Evangeline's cloaking spells, we practically flew there in less than three hours. Every few miles, Evangeline dialed Ben's number again but she never got through. By the time we saw the city sign, she was on the verge of a breakdown.

Traveling from Seattle proper into the haven was a breeze

when going on foot. In a car, things got a little more complicated. One person slipping into an enchanted doorway was easy to hide in plain sight. No one suspected anything. Hiding the fact that an entire car disappears is a much more difficult feat and requires more planning.

Luckily, Adam knew what to do. He maneuvered down a few side streets and we shot out onto a road that wound along the waterfront, away from the sparkle and glow of downtown. A few minutes later, we arrived at the shipping docks. It was dark and he slowed down to carefully consider his next turn down a long driveway. We pulled up to an iron-barred security gate and Adam rolled down the window and typed in a code.

The gate lurched and shuddered open. He waited until it was completely clear to creep forward, his eyes scanning the dark outlines of the storage units. Light fixtures were dispersed throughout the rows of cement buildings, but somehow got swallowed up in the darkness of the night. Adam carefully counted off the gates of the different units. When he reached the one he was looking for he idled, staring at the door. "All right, ladies. It's now or never."

"Where are we?" Evangeline asked from the back seat.

"This is the portal into the haven when traveling by car."

"Should I get out and open the door?" I asked, peering up at the solid structure.

Without a reply Adam slammed his foot on the gas. The car leapt forward toward the door. I yelped and squeezed my eyes closed. "Adam!"

I waited for the crash but it didn't come.

Adam let out a victorious *whoop* and I peeled my eyes open one at a time, then breathed a sigh of relief when I realized what had happened. The storage unit *was* the portal. "Stars!" I exclaimed.

Evangeline gasped. "I thought you'd lost your mind!"

Adam laughed. "Not yet!"

I laughed and we started down the street that had opened up before us. It wasn't familiar, but as we drove on, it became obvious where the portal had spat us out; we were a few miles outside of the main hub of the haven. After about a mile, we reached a fork. To the left was the haven. To the right, a highway led to the suburban area inhabited by those who worked in the haven but didn't want to live in the trendy condos or apartments.

"Still nothing," Evangeline announced after attempting yet again to get Ben on the phone. "It's been hours. Where could he be?"

"Hopefully at Sasha's," I said. "Considering we've come all this way."

"Well even if Ben isn't, eventually *she* will be," Adam pointed out, taking a right turn. "I think it's time we introduced ourselves."

We drove in silence for a while. I rolled down my window and let in some of the cool night breeze. My nerves weren't completely soothed, but the brisk air helped some.

"Here we go," Adam said, finally breaking the silence as we turned onto a side street that fed into an upscale neighborhood.

I whistled low under my breath. "Apparently being a council member comes with a pretty fat salary," I noted, staring at the hulking outlines of the massive houses lining the street.

Most of them had lights on in one or more rooms but Sasha's was a bright beacon. From the street, it looked as though every light in the house had been turned on. Was she having some kind of party? There weren't any cars in the driveway in front of the garage. Curtains blocked the view into the front room of the house, but I thought I could see flutters of shadows on the other side.

Evangeline started to open her door. "Ready?"

"Wait, wait," Adam said. "We don't know what's going on in there."

"Or who she's with," I added.

The answer came seconds later. Evangeline closed her door again and Adam killed the headlights. Orbs of light hovered along the street, casting bright, blueish light over the sidewalk. We all stared, faces pressed to the windows, as a trio of people walked down the sidewalk and up the front steps of Sasha's house.

Adam leaned closer. "Those kind of look like—"

"Vamps," I said.

"Bat wings."

"Vampires?" Evangeline said.

The trio reached the front door and stood under the porch lights. Angular features, dark, glittering eyes, and—

"Definitely vamps," I said, startled when one threw his head back, laughing at something the other had said, and revealed long fangs.

"What is a witch doing throwing a house party for a bunch of vamps?" Adam asked.

Sasha came to the door and invited the three in, a cruel smile on her face.

Before I could even attempt to scrape together an explanation, another group of lanky party-goers waltzed up the front steps.

"Is this really happening?" I said, watching vampire after vampire walk up the front steps.

Adam turned over the engine and the zippy little car purred to life. "I think we need to go. We can't storm a house full of vampires and expect to walk away alive. We'll go back to the manor. You can call that agent you know, Bramble, and send her over here to figure this out."

He put the car in reverse, preparing to leave, but I lashed out and gripped his arm tightly. "Wait!"

"Holly?"

I jabbed my finger at the window. He followed my icy stare up the front walk of the well-groomed yard and saw Ben standing in the front window, peeking through the curtains. His eyes glowed yellow, a flicker of something else lurking underneath the surface of his handsome face.

"We gotta go!" Adam hissed.

∽

WE WAITED for the curtains to fall closed again and then Adam hit the gas. He flicked the headlights on after we were a few blocks away from the house.

"We're leaving him there?" Evangeline asked, craning around in her seat to look out the back windshield.

Adam sighed. "Evie, there's nothing we can do. If he's in real danger, why would he have been standing there at the window? He looked like more of a guard dog if you ask me."

"He's a werewolf in a house full of vampires!" she objected.

"Not all vampires hate werewolves," I replied. "Lacey doesn't."

Even as I said it, a million questions of my own swirled through my head.

Evangeline gave up arguing by the time we went back through the portal into Seattle proper and headed back to Beechwood Harbor. Adam picked up the speed even more as we flew down the highway back to the coast. By the time we got back to the manor, it was creeping up on midnight and I was more confused and exhausted than I had been in quite some time. I was ready to have a cup of tea and go to bed.

Posy floated through the ceiling as we all trooped inside.

DANIELLE GARRETT

She greeted us and then gestured at a large bank box sitting off to one side of the entryway. "That came for you earlier, dear. I had Lacey bring it in before she left for the night."

"What is it?" I asked, not expecting an answer. I kicked out of my boots and went to inspect the box. "It's from Harriet. These must be the files Teddy asked for, Or at least copies. I imagine the SPA isn't willing to part with the originals."

"Should I wake Teddy up?" Evangeline asked. "I'm sure he'd be eager to see these."

"No," I replied. "Let him sleep. We're not going to solve anything tonight. I just want to take a quick peek." I crossed my legs and started digging through the stacks of papers. "Looks like this top section is notes and photos from the SPA raid at Raven."

I flipped through some of the images. It was strange to think it had all happened only six weeks before. So much had happened since. One image showed Harvey, reading a vampire his rights at the side of the transport van.

Adam and Evangeline sat beside me and helped dig through the contents. "I wonder if she found anything that will help your hearing," Adam said.

I reached the bottom of the stack and was about to put it back into the box when another image caught my attention. My heart slammed against my ribs as I reached for the photo with shaking fingers.

"You guys ...," My hand trembled, sending ripples through the photo as I lifted it. "Look at the name on this one."

Adam took the page from me. His mouth dropped open. "Carlotta Pringle? As in—?"

"It has to be!" I stared at the picture. "She looks like a clone of Sasha! Adam, that listing you found said her mother's name was Marla."

"Could this be her aunt?" Adam asked. He dug his phone

out of his pocket and started typing frantically. "We just added new pages to the database. Let me see ..."

After a few tense moments, he shook his head. "You're not going to believe this."

"Try me."

"No one named Marla Pringle has ever lived inside the haven system."

"Which means she doesn't exist." I shook my head. "Not if she was married to a council member. She wouldn't have been able to stay out of the haven life."

Adam ran a hand through his hair. "So that means her mother must be ..."

"Wait. Wait." Evangeline frowned. "What are you saying? That Sasha is some kind of witch-vampire? Is that even possible?"

I shook my head and stared at the woman in the processing photo. "If you had asked me yesterday, I would have said no. But now ... after seeing this?"

"Guess that explains the little shindig at her place tonight," Adam said as he inspected the photo. "Dead-ringer if you ask me."

"Her mother is a vampire and was arrested in the raid on Raven." I reeled back as though a board had smacked me in the face. "That's why she hates me! I'm the one who told the SPA about the Vampire Council. I'm the reason that raid even happened!"

No one argued with me. Adam and Evangeline stared at one another, not blinking.

"No wonder she wants to ruin my life. She thinks I'm the one responsible for her mother getting arrested and trucked off to some SPA prison."

"Surely if her daughter served on the council she could wiggle out of it," Evangeline said.

"Not if she doesn't want anyone to know who her mother

is. Right now, everyone thinks her mother's name is Marla. No one knows the truth."

Another jolt of recognition hit me. I stared down at the picture. I flipped it over. There, in big black letters: *Sasha Pringle???*

My heart sank to the bottom of my stomach. "No one except Harvey."

CHAPTER 22

Frantic pounding on the manor's front door ripped me from a deep sleep. Boots sat up in bed, his ears tilted forward, on full alert. "What in the Otherworld?" I mumbled sleepily to myself.

Boots growled and I sat up beside him, my eyes working overtime to adjust to the darkness.

"What is it, Boots?" I looked over at the glowing clock on my bedside table. It was past midnight.

A thump sounded as Boots jumped to the floor. I jumped from the bed, slid my feet into my waiting pair of slippers, and grabbed the robe off the top of my dresser on my way to the door. It was open a crack and Boots pushed it open wider as he left. In the hall, he let out another low growl.

The hairs on the back of my neck stood up.

More pounding. Louder this time.

I craned around to look up the darkened staircase. I wanted Adam at my side but I also didn't want whoever was at the door to wake up the entire household. Especially if it was Nick with more questions. I didn't want to start *that* conversation all over again.

Boots was at my feet when I pulled the door open. I straightened, surprised, when I realized it was Ben. In the yellow glow of the porch lights, his face looked sallow. His brow was covered in sweat as though he'd run several miles. "Holly! I saw you tonight. You have to help me!"

"What's wrong, Ben?" I tightened the sash on my robe against the chill pouring in through the front door.

Boots brushed past my leg and planted himself between me and Ben. I glanced down at him and saw he was glaring up at Ben. I nudged him with my foot. He wasn't a huge fan of strangers—especially not ones who had anything to do with dogs or large, predatory animals. The fact that he'd accepted Adam was nothing short of a miracle.

"Listen, I don't know what exactly you've gotten yourself into, but as someone who's been around the so-called Vampire Council, I would advise you to run fast and run far."

Ben's face shifted. He lunged forward and caught me by the shoulders. "You have to help me, Holly! I barely got away from her!"

Boots hissed and took a swipe at Ben.

Get Adam! Boots, go, get, Adam!

"Ben, please, let me go," I said. Boots reluctantly backed up, turned, and bolted for the stairs.

"She's a killer, Holly!"

I tried to take a step back but Ben's grip on my shoulders only tightened. "I don't know what you're talking about, Ben. Please, just let me go. We can talk! I promise I'll listen to anything you have to say!"

Ben's eyes flashed, suddenly glowing like red-hot embers in a campfire. His head twisted to the side so violently I almost expected to hear a snap. I sucked in a quick breath and then dared to look away to see what had so capture his attention.

My heart stopped cold.

No. It couldn't be.

Nick was across the street. He was stopped at the corner of the neighborhood, his hands stuffed inside the pockets of his thick winter jacket.

Ben snarled and released me with a violent shove. I heard fabric tear. Ben lunged down the sidewalk, loping like a half-beast. I glanced down at myself; the shoulders of my coat had been torn to shreds.

His fingers had turned into claws. Claws that carried the dark and twisted were curse.

"Nick, run!" I screamed. The boom of my voice bounced off the dark outlines of the neighboring houses and returned to me. My pulse skittered into a frantic rhythm, and for a moment I thought it might explode from my chest. "Nick, *run!*"

Nick turned and ran but Ben was closing the distance, moving too quickly.

Nick was in good shape but wouldn't be able to outpace him. I surged forward, hands raised as magic sprang to my fingertips. With a cry, the spell ripped from me and surged toward Ben, a stream of red and blue sparks. The spell hit him and he lurched to one side.

Ben scrambled to get back on two legs and then tore off again.

"Ben! Stop this!"

If he heard me, it didn't faze him. He got his feet under him and plowed forward. I tried another stunning spell. It missed.

"Holly!" Evangeline's voice cut through the pounding of my pulse in my ears.

I whipped around and saw her on the manor's front steps. She had her wand raised, a light coming from the tip filled the yard. "What in the Otherworld is going on?"

Boots streaked past her legs. A huge black dog followed.

Adam looked up at me, his eyes even darker in his beast-form. "Ben! He's after Nick!"

Adam launched himself from the porch, his huge toenails sending chunks of wood flying.

Posy was going to kill us all.

Adam tore into the night, Boots on his heels. Evangeline jumped down the steps and we raced after them.

With the help of the powerful beam of light from Evangeline's wand, I could see all the way down the steep hill that led from the center of town up to the bluff where the manor and neighboring houses stood. Adam and Boots were gaining on Ben as he loped around the corner where the residential sidewalk stopped and the main strip through town started.

Where was Nick?

For once, I envied Lacey. She had supernatural speed and could have covered the distance in a split second. As it was, I couldn't seem to make my feet move fast enough—of course, it didn't help that I was wearing bedroom slippers from last Christmas that were a size too large.

"What does he want with Nick?" Evangeline panted as we ran into town.

"I don't think it was personal." My heart raced all the more as I remembered the way his eyes had glowed and how quickly his head had snapped around when he'd scented Nick. "He's changing into the wolf!"

Evangeline didn't ask anything else but her pace quickened.

We rounded the corner and slammed to a stop. Both of our heads swiveled frantically but there was no sign of any of them. I hoped that meant Adam and Boots had caught up with Ben before he got to Nick.

My hope shattered when a horrifying scream sounded from a bit farther ahead.

The sound echoed and clanged in my ears. My legs, quivering and weak, kicked back into motion. I skittered around the corner of the alley and peered into the darkness. Without thinking, I threw my hand into the darkness and sent a shower of sparks overhead in a wide arc. It was just enough light to make sense of the scene before me. Nick was pinned, his back flattened against a wall, a dark figure towering over him. Ben. My mouth opened, ready to hurl a powerful spell, but it was a sliver of a second too late. Ben's clawed, half-paw, half-human hand came down with a powerful swipe. Nick cried out and tried to push Ben off of him but Ben didn't so much as flinch.

I couldn't tear my eyes away from the wound on Nick's chest. Time froze, a snapshot of terror and dread, before Nick bellowed again, furious and in pain. The sound jarred me from the paralysis that gripped me and my vision tunneled. The buildings on either side of the alley blurred and all I could see was Nick and the half-beast pinning him. The spell shot from my mouth like a cannon ball and blasted into Ben. He roared, the sound primal and dangerous. Every hair on my arms and neck rose in response to the eerie sound. Ben faltered, stumbling back, but didn't fall completely to the ground. Nick scrambled back as the ring of lights started to fade. I hurried to shoot up a new flurry of lights, higher this time to signal for help, and then barreled forward to catch Nick as he swayed in place.

"Nick!" My eyes swept over him frantically. The pain was evident on his face. The wounds were deep and blood pooled on the front of his shirt. "We have to get you out of here."

"Holly! Nick!" Evangeline caught up to me and her wand drenched the alley in light. I turned and saw Ben, crouched on all fours along the opposite wall. His low growl filled the alley and vibrated through me. I raised my hand, ready to strike him again but stopped when I realized he wasn't looking in our direction. He was distracted. His body was morphing and changing before my eyes. From the look on his face—pained and tight—it wasn't pleasant.

Good.

"Is he okay? What happened?" Evangeline asked, her voice laced with panic.

I ignored her long enough to set a protective ward around Nick. "Nick, stay right there. You're safe. No matter what you see, you're protected. You have to trust me. Don't move! I'm going to get help."

He nodded but then his head lolled back against the brick wall. His chest was rising and falling too fast.

"Nick, breathe," I said, keeping my voice soft. "It's going to be all right."

Nick moaned and a fresh stab of pain bit into me. I looked at Evangeline. "Ben—" I paused and sucked in a gulp of air. "Ben got him."

Evangeline's eyes went wide. Her mouth opened and closed, then opened again although she couldn't get anything out. She hand against her mouth and shook her head. "No," she mumbled through her fingers. "No. No."

"There's a protective ward around Nick. When I get Ben out of here, break the ward and get Nick to the manor," I told Evangeline out of the corner of my mouth. I couldn't risk taking my eyes off the wolf for even a second.

Across the alley Ben lifted his strange face—his nose transforming into a long, full muzzle—and dark fur sprouted from everywhere. It was like watching plants grow on some kind of time-lapse video. It happened all at once. One minute, pale skin. The next, dark fur covering every inch. His yellow eyes were no longer glowing, but looked just as deadly as they had on the porch.

"Holly, no," Evangeline protested, stooping down to tend to Nick. "You can't ask that of me!"

"You have to," I said firmly. "I can't have anything else

happen to Nick. Promise me, Evangeline. Promise me you'll get him out of here."

I shifted, positioning myself to spring up and make a run for it. I didn't have a specific plan in mind. All I knew was I needed to get Ben to chase me and give Evangeline and Nick enough time to escape.

"I promise, Holly. But please, don't—"

A second, familiar growl sounded, and relief rushed through me.

"Adam!"

The huge black dog burst into sight at the mouth of the alley and my heart slammed against my ribs so hard I thought it might become permanently bruised. He surged forward and used his body as a barrier between us and Ben. I pushed to my feet and looked at Ben again. His body was still mid-change, his hands and feet transformed into huge paws. Judging by the size of them, when he was fully wolf, he would be tough for even Adam to take on by himself.

What in the Otherworld were we supposed to do? Civilized werewolves had a plan, a place to change where they wouldn't hurt anyone. They'd go into the mountains or lock themselves in a cement-encased room. Even if Adam could win the fight with Ben, what would we do then? He couldn't kill him. He wasn't some animal. He was a person. Our one-time friend.

Ben's eyes locked onto Adam and he snarled. Long, three-inch canines peeked out from his dripping jowls. Adam replied with his own low, menacing growl.

Were they communicating?

Boots raced around Adam and burrowed into Nick.

"Evangeline, go! Get him to the manor! Tell Lacey what's happening. Call Agent Bramble. Wake up the whole SPA! Tell them there's a werewolf on the loose and that Sasha Pringle is behind it!"

Without waiting for her to agree, I raised my hand and sent another blasting spell into Ben's side. He slammed back into the wall, stunned for a moment.

Evangeline hauled Nick to his feet as gently as she could and led him from the alley.

"Boots, go with them," I said as his amber eyes swiveled up at me. He hesitated. "Go!"

The spell wore off too quickly. My magic was dwindling. Every spell was harder to bring forth. It was like digging for water at the bottom of a near-empty well—I was getting less and less with each scoop. I couldn't hold out much longer. If I pushed things too far, I'd end up collapsing, turning myself into a liability instead of an asset.

Ben pushed up to his feet and stood fully. He swiped a large paw at Adam, who reeled back and then lunged forward. Loud sirens sounded in the background and I realized all the commotion had likely woken up half of Beechwood Harbor. Panic seized me, but I sagged back against the brick wall. My breathing was ragged and frantic, coming in like wheezes.

Adam stood on his own hind legs and pressed Ben against the wall. He growled low and looked over his hulking shoulder at me.

"What are we going to do with him? We can't let him loose! There're way too many humans around," I asked, my voice frantic.

Adam couldn't speak in beast form. He kept him pinned against the wall and stared at me. He'd be no match for him once Ben fully changed. We had to hurry.

"We're going to have to lock him up somewhere." I racked my brain. But where? The manor didn't have a basement. The greenhouse was too easy to break out of. None of the bedrooms would hold him.

Ben's eyes flashed again. There was something different

about it this time. It wasn't the urge to hunt. Or anger. It was fear.

Panic flared inside me, rising quickly and then bursting like a firework. My whole body trembled from the effect. I ground my teeth together to keep them from chattering and turned to Adam.

Before I could get out another word, the reason behind the fear in Ben's eyes became clear.

A cold chill snapped at my bare legs, then a burst of green flashed.

I closed my eyes against the bright light and when I opened them again, Sasha Pringle was standing at the mouth of the alley.

CHAPTER 23

"There you are!"

Sasha's voice raked over my skin like a thousand pins digging in all at once.

"And it looks like you've made some friends," she added, her voice cold. "Good dog."

Ben lowered his head, an almost reverent gesture. Sasha snapped her fingers and blasted Adam away from Ben. The wolf loped forward to stand at Sasha's side. Adam rallied and leaped forward, propelling himself off his massive haunches. He bared his teeth at Sasha, a crazy look in his dark eyes.

Sasha laughed. "Nice try, mutt."

With a casual flick of her wrist, a blast of light surged from her palm and slammed into Adam. He hit the brick wall with a yelp and crumpled to the ground, whimpering.

"Adam!" I lunged forward, only to be swept aside by a powerful whip of a spell. I gasped at the impact and fell backward.

Ben cowered at his mistress's feet, fully wolf. Standing tall, he would have reached her hip but with his posture tucked he was only half that size.

What kind of hold did she have over him?

"See, Holly, if you're going to run with dogs, you have to teach them to respect you," Sasha said with a twisted smile as she looked over at Adam's limp body. "I'll let you in on a little secret: it's easier if they fear you."

Every fiber of my being was urging me to go to Adam's side, but I knew there was no way Sasha would let me get close. I didn't even know if he was breathing, but I didn't dare take my eyes off Sasha. Magic danced on her palm as she watched me. My own fingertips felt like they were on fire, every drop of my remaining magic pooling rapidly. I wouldn't get more than one final shot. I'd used too much of it fighting Ben.

The sirens in the background were growing louder. The police station wasn't far from where we stood. It would be mere seconds before the police—the *human* police—were in the line of Sasha's wrath.

She cocked her head at the sound. "And here I thought we might have a private chat."

"You need to go, Sasha! I won't let you hurt anyone tonight."

She laughed. "I'm not done with you, Holly Boldt. But you're right. I don't need humans mucking up my plans." She raised her hands and a green shield surrounded us. For a moment I thought it was a ward or some kind of cloak, but then a blast of heat seared through me.

My eyes squeezed tight against the pain, then in a flash, it was gone.

When I pried my eyes open, everything was different. Sasha and Ben were there, their postures unchanged, but we were no longer in the middle of Beechwood Harbor, and Adam was nowhere to be seen. I could only hope Evangeline had found them before the human police did, and that they were both alive.

We were surrounded by trees and it didn't take me long to realize we were in the woods behind the manor. Deep in the woods. Far enough away that I couldn't even see the lights from the house.

My heart pounded in my ears as a new, disparaging fear gripped me. What kind of magic had she used? It was unlike anything I'd seen, or even heard of before.

The shimmering green light sparkled out, leaving only the light from the half-moon and the scattering of stars peeking through the treetops. Sasha looked even more terrifying with her face bathed in starlight.

Ben whimpered and she kicked him. He yelped and sunk lower to the ground, nearly on his belly.

"Why do you need a werewolf?" I asked, snapping my eyes to hers. "What do you want with Ben? He obviously doesn't want to be anywhere near you!"

"Ben here owes me a debt," she replied with a disdainful look down at the lowly wolf. "Isn't that right?"

Ben didn't move or even lift his eyes.

"See, he got into some trouble with a few of my friends. So I cursed him. Once he's paid his debt, I'll release him from the curse. Simple as that."

"You cursed him into changing mid-moon?" I spat, trying not to let my jaw hit the ground.

Sasha laughed as though it wasn't a serious question. As though dynamically changing the effect of an ancient curse was mere child's play, something first-year academy students could perform with their eyes closed. "As long as he's in my debt, he will continue to change whenever I see fit. If he keeps me happy and does what I ask, we don't have any problems."

"Until tonight," I said with a triumphant grin. "He got away from you!"

Sasha tilted her head. "Yes, and he will pay for that slip in judgment. Maybe I'll leave him this way forever."

Ben whined.

"What were you thinking?" she asked the wolf. "You thought *she* was your best shot?" Sasha threw her head back and laughed as though it were the funniest joke in the world. A shiver threaded down my spine as the moonlight glinted off her fangs.

So it was true. She was half witch and half vampire.

If Harvey knew—or at least strongly suspected—the truth, why hadn't he had her investigated? Surely he would have uncovered the ties to the Vampire Council. How had she managed to be on the council for my hearing? Was that why he'd left? He hadn't expected her to be there?

Sasha took a calculated step closer, her mouth twisted into a wicked grin. "See, what Ben didn't realize is that the reason I had him spying on you wasn't because I was worried about you being a threat. Instead, it was a way for me to plot out the best moment to get rid of you. Just like I did with your little goblin friend, Harvey." She laughed again. "This isn't ideal timing, but it will have to do. I supposed I'll have to make sure there isn't enough of you left over for the SPA to find, since I don't have time to find some stooge to glamour into doing the dirty work for me."

My eyes widened. "You glamoured Dune Kasey into poisoning Harvey?"

"Aren't you a clever little witch," she said sarcastically. "If only you hadn't wasted so much time chasing after Praxle and Mache."

My heart sank, realizing my mistake.

Sasha threw her head back and laughed again. "Honestly, what were you thinking? Those two combined barely have an IQ high enough to keep their own scheme running, let alone plot a murder."

So they *were* in cahoots, just not on this.

"You're smarter than most, I suppose. At least you made the connection." She cocked her hip and considered me. "Maybe you'd be of better use to me alive." She looked down at Ben. "What do you think? You need a partner? Or would you rather have a chew toy?"

"If you think I'd do anything to help you after what you did to Harvey, then you're the stupid one!" I exclaimed, disgusted. "You killed him just because he discovered what you are!"

"What I *am* is the most powerful witch you've ever met." Sasha's eyes flashed. A stream of light flung from her hand and whipped at my shins. "Have some respect, Holly. I'm trying to offer you a way out."

Magic tingled along my palms. I called for more. Dug deeper and deeper. I'd get one shot. I had to make it count.

"See, Holly, I wasn't going to kill you at first. I just wanted to keep you out of my way. But you proved to be more of a nuisance than I expected. When Ben reported that you were digging into the investigation and throwing around wild claims about Mache and Praxle, I knew you weren't going to drop it and had to take matters into my own hands."

I looked at Ben, still cowering at her feet. A flash of a memory surged back to me; the request for more hand salve. What about the day Evangeline and I told Lucy everything that was going on? Had he heard everything from behind the curtain?

He didn't look me in the eye.

"How did you know Harvey would leave my hearing? How did Dune know to follow him when he was supposed to be in Council Hall?"

"I had Ben call Harvey that day you were in court. He lured him into Seattle. From Ben's surveillance, I knew he got a coffee whenever he passed through the portal at that human-infested coffee shop. All Dune had to do was slip him the potion."

From there, he'd gotten into a cab, and by the time the potion went to work, the driver abandoned the cab in that alley way. The SPA hadn't yet found the driver—the only witness to Harvey's final moments.

Sasha gave me a knowing smile. "It didn't take much to convince Dune. He was already more than willing to attack Harvey. All I did was facilitate the when and how of it all. And sure, maybe gave him a little *nudge*."

I reared back at the coldness in her voice.

She found my expression amusing. "With Harvey out of the way, my secret would remain safe and I could convince my fellow council members to release my mother without exposing who she was."

"What? You were going to glamour all the other members?"

She gave a slight shrug. "It worked in your hearing, didn't it?"

My mouth dropped open as the final pieces of the puzzle clicked into place, and the rage gave me a little extra boost of power.

I'd dragged up as much magic as I possibly could and even with the boost, I'd never felt so drained before.

Sasha caught the glint of magic as it surged to the surface. She grinned. "You think you can win this fight, Holly? Maybe you're not as smart as Harvey thought."

I threw my hands forward, aiming right for the sneer on her face. The blast of magic ripped from me and I stumbled forward at the effort. Every drop flew toward Sasha. She took a step to the side but at the last second, Ben lunged up and pushed her directly into the path. Sasha was thrust into the spell like a rag doll. Surprise registered on her face just as it hit her full-blast. She froze in place for a few silent seconds, shock etched on her face, and then crumpled to the ground. Ben yelped as the magical blast grazed him, and he fell beside her.

The world went sideways and I dropped to my knees in the cold, wet grass. I dug my fingers into the ground, desperate for something to hold onto.

A loud screech pierced the sky. Hope surged inside me, and I looked up, expecting to see Evangeline's familiar, Flurry, a hawk, sent to find me. He could lead me back to the manor. When I looked up, my heart sank. The dark shadow against the moon wasn't Flurry. This bird was three times as big, the sharp talons extended in a menacing gesture.

Was this Sasha's familiar? It certainly fit.

My magic was depleted. Completely dried up. I wouldn't have been able to light a pile of fresh kindling if my life depended on it. With my options limited, I tried to get to my feet and lurched for cover behind a tree.

The eagle's sharp eyes locked with mine right before it dive-bombed. I screamed and instinctively tried to avoid it, only to realize half a heartbeat later who it was, and that the massive bird was on my side. It veered past me and landed on the ground.

"Agent Bramble!"

She stood before me, fully shifted back into her human form. Apparently—and thankfully—she had mastered the ability to shift with her clothing intact, as not a single wrinkle or loose thread was evident on her hounds-tooth suit. It suddenly dawned on me who she reminded me of: Posy. She was a living, breathing incarnation of Posy.

Granted, a fiercer, kicking-butt-and-taking-names version, but the resemblance was definitely there.

Agent Bramble raced forward, her eyes sweeping over the scene, not missing a detail. She rounded on me after ensuring that Sasha and Ben were down. "Your friend called me. She said there was a werewolf in Beechwood Harbor. I flew here as fast as I could and when I was nearing Beechwood Harbor I saw a flash of green. What happened here?"

I sagged against the tree, drained of every ounce of energy. I barely managed to meet her eyes.

Bramble gave me some space while she made a series of phone calls. When backup was on the way, she inspected the bodies. "They're both still breathing," she said.

I breathed deeply, somehow relieved. It hadn't been my intention to kill either of them, but the blast had been furious, and from the way they landed, I hadn't been sure. My mind reeled back to the way Adam's form had looked in the alley way.

"Agent Bramble?" I called as loudly as I could, still only managing a puff of a whisper. "Adam?"

"Your roommate, Evangeline, said he was attacked but he's unharmed."

Relief washed over me and I sank into blessed darkness.

When I awoke, the scene before me was crawling with SPA agents. Agent Bramble hovered nearby and was the first to notice I was awake. I moved stiffly, but at least I'd regained a little energy.

"Stay there, Holly. You need to rest." She squatted beside me. "Can you tell me, step by step, exactly what happened?"

I nodded and then licked my lips, ready to purge the events of the horrible night.

When I finished recounting the details of the evening, she looked at me, a combination of sympathy and admiration etched on her face. "You've had quite a night."

She asked few questions, but took diligent notes

throughout my recounting. She closed her notebook and frowned at me. "I'm sorry for what you've gone through tonight, Holly. Truly. Is there anything I can do to help?"

"I just want to go home."

She smiled wanly. "That I can do."

CHAPTER 24

Bone-tired and freezing cold, I practically fell through the front door of the manor. Lacey shot up from her place on the couch beside Nick. He lay curled into a tight ball and though his lips moved, he didn't open his eyes. Her grave expression answered the question on my lips before I could ask it. "Any changes?"

She shook her head. "He's still out."

"Thanks for staying with him," I told her.

"Sure." She looked back down at Nick. "Do you think he'll be okay?"

I shrugged helplessly. I didn't have an answer for her.

"Where is everyone else?" I asked. "Adam and Evangeline?"

"They went back out to look for you. Adam's out searching. Evangeline and Teddy took her car. I think they said something about Seattle."

My eyes slid shut. "How long ago?"

"Twenty minutes, maybe. They stayed to take care of Nick first. Evangeline cleaned the wound and bandaged him up before she gave him one of your teas. I assumed it was to help him sleep."

"Let's hope she got the dose right this time," I said with a faint smile. "I'll call Adam."

I slipped into the kitchen and dialed Evangeline's phone. She answered with a frantic *hello* on the first ring. I told her I was back at the manor and after assuring her half a dozen times I was all right, she said she and Teddy would turn around at the next exit and head home. They'd been heading toward Seattle.

After hanging up, I went to the back porch and yelled for Adam, hoping he would hear me and come back to the manor. When he didn't appear, I went back to the living room to check on Nick.

Posy hovered nervously over Nick. "I'm so sorry, dear. I'm glad you're all right though."

"Thank you." I stared at Nick as Lacey pulled a blanket over him.

"Will he have the curse?" I finally dared to ask.

Lacey was the one who answered. "He's no longer human."

My heart sank at the finality of both her words and tone. She was right. There was no point in arguing or holding out hope that somehow the inevitable might be prevented. I'd seen the gashes across Nick's chest. They were made from claws. No doubt about it. And while my werewolf knowledge was limited, any witch or wizard who had been even partially awake during academy would know that all it took to pass the curse from a were to a human were scratches or a bite during the change.

Nick would live, but his life would never be the same.

Adam arrived home at the same time Evangeline and Teddy pulled back in the driveway along the side of the manor. He raced inside, threw a blanket around his waist, and clutched me tightly against his chest. His expression was a tangled mess of rage and relief. Tears streamed down my face when I realized how scared he'd been. "I'm sorry, Adam," I finally whispered.

"You can't do that ever again, Holly," he said, his voice tense. "Chasing after a werewolf in the middle of the night?"

"It was stupid. I didn't know what else to do, though."

He held me tighter.

"I can't lose you, gorgeous," he said into my hair.

I met his eyes. "Adam—" my throat swelled, choking out the rest.

He kissed me and then took my hand and led me into the kitchen where Evangeline was waiting, a fresh pot of coffee nearly finished brewing. It was going to be a long night.

After I'd explained everything that had happened following my jump with Sasha, we rejoined Lacey and Posy in the living room. It took a few hours for Nick to wake up but when he finally started to come around, we moved him to the sitting room off the foyer. If needed, it would be easier to keep him contained, as the sitting room had heavy wooden doors that could be locked. Of course, a werewolf in full change could eventually bust through them or dive out one of the picture windows lining the room. However, short of chaining him up in the attic, it was the best option we had.

When Nick opened his eyes, I was sitting at his side. His eyes fluttered a few times and then went wide, his pupils turning to tiny specks. When his pinpoint pupils found me, a flicker of relief washed over his face. "Holly," he said, slightly dazed.

"You're okay, Nick," I started. His forehead was damp

with sweat. I motioned to Evangeline and quietly asked if she could bring a cloth and she slipped from the room.

"What happened?" Nick asked me. His eyes never wavered, even to where Adam stood, hovering behind me. The bright blue orbs stayed locked on my face, unblinking. Desperation rolled from him in near palpable waves. He knew something was horribly, horribly wrong and he was waiting for me to tell him he was right. He was silently pleading with me to tell him the truth, something I should have done a long time ago. No matter how awful. I wondered if it was similar to how military nurses and doctors felt, working on the freshly wounded, straight off the battlefield. How did they do it? How did they look into those wide-eyed faces and tell them the worst?

I drew in a silent breath. "Do you remember anything from last night?"

"I came to see you. It was late. Maybe close to midnight. I couldn't sleep so I got dressed and went for a walk. Sometimes a long walk gets me tired enough that I don't have the strange dreams. I didn't really intend to come see you, but I wound up at the manor. I thought maybe someone would be awake but the lights were all turned off. I turned around to go home."

I cringed, wishing I'd been awake. If he'd been safely inside the manor, then he wouldn't have the marred wounds on his chest.

"I don't know what happened after that. Or, at least," he paused and looked up at me. "The things I remember don't make sense."

"Nick, there's so much I have to say, I don't really know where to start ..."

I trailed off and slowly shook my head.

Nick reached out and took my hand. I met his pleading eyes. "Holly, just tell me the truth. Am I losing my mind or is something weird going on? I trust you, Holly, with my friendship, my life. Please, just tell me the truth."

Tears pooled in the corners of my eyes. I had no idea what or how to explain it all to Nick, but I had promised myself I wouldn't cry. I sniffed and blinked quickly to clear them away before they could fall.

Adam squeezed my shoulder and then left the room, closing the door behind him.

I shifted my focus back to Nick and with a quick nod, I started the tale. "You're not going crazy."

Something unreadable passed through Nick's eyes, and in that moment I had no idea what he'd hoped the answer would be. Had he wanted me to tell him he was losing his mind? Would that have been an easier pill to swallow? Perhaps, but it wasn't the one he could have. Not anymore.

"Nick, I'm a witch. A *real* witch."

His mouth moved but no sounds came out. Finally he squeezed his eyes shut, gave his head a shake, and then tried again. "Like *Harry Potter* or something?"

I laughed softly. "Something like that."

It took close to two hours to explain everything: the haven system, different types of supernaturals, and what had actually happened the night of the SPA raid on Raven. He asked a lot of questions along the way, and when the crash course in all things supernatural came to an end, he shifted his eyes to the coffered ceiling of the living room and tried to absorb it all. I sat with him, not saying a word, until he finally turned to look at me. "Does everyone else know?"

"Here in the manor?"

He nodded.

Right. I'd given a crash course on supernatural creatures 101 but had left out the multitude of them in Beechwood Harbor.

Nick tried to sit up, but grimaced and sank back down.

"Is everyone in Beechwood magic? Am I in some weird *Twilight Zone*? Of all the cities …"

I cringed. "Not everyone in Beechwood, no. But in this house … yes."

"Evangaline?"

"She's a witch. Yes."

"Lacey?"

"Vamp."

His eyes went wide. "Adam?"

"Shifter."

He blinked twice. "Who else? Cassie? Chief?"

"No, and no." I shook my head. "Let's see, there's Lucy at the spa, she's a telepath."

"She can read minds?"

"Not anymore," I answered. "She's medicated."

Nick's eyebrows rose another half an inch. I worried he was creating permanent wrinkles in his forehead.

"Oh, right, I forgot that part. I'm a potions witch. That's my specialty. I used to sell my potions all over town, in fact."

Nick gave his head a shake. I wondered if he hoped his mind was like an Etch-a-Sketch, so he could shake it and clear away all the disturbing information I'd dumped on him.

I inclined my head. "There's one more thing," I said, bracing myself.

He gave a crooked smile. "I'm not sure how much more I can process."

"I understand." I chewed on my lower lip for a moment, wondering if I should insist or let him have some time to sort out what he already knew. I had no idea what would happen to him. I'd never known a werewolf right after he'd been cursed. Would there be immediate physical changes? Or would Nick remain normal until the full moon? Should I lock him in a room just to be safe?

Finally I broke my silence. "I know this is a lot, but I really don't think this can wait."

"Okay?"

I sighed. "Nick, last night you were attacked."

He looked down at his bare chest at the large bandage Evangeline had applied after I'd treated the wound with a healing salve that I'd mixed up fresh—haven rules be damned. "Well I didn't figure this was a new fashion trend," he said with a grimace.

"When you were walking home last night, you drew some unwanted attention from a werewolf." I lowered my eyes to the bandage. A flicker of pain flared in my chest. I would have given everything I owned to take the scratches away, to make the nightmare end. "He's the one who gave you that wound."

I couldn't make myself say the words but Nick's face morphed from confusion to pure terror. He threw the blanket off from his waist and jumped up from the couch. He yelped at the pain but didn't stop moving. He tore across the room in three wide bounds.

"Nick!" I hurried to his side but he threw an arm up, blocking me from touching him.

The tears I'd tried to keep away came hot and fast at the twisted pain and fear on his face. "It's going to be okay," I forced myself to say through the sobs. "We're going to fix it—"

"How?" he demanded, his voice booming through the entire manor.

I blinked, surprised by the power.

"I'm a monster now!" he spat. "You just said as much!"

Adam pushed back into the room, his posture that of a riled dog. "What's going on?" His dark, almost black, eyes shot from me to Nick and then back to me.

Nick rounded on Adam and for a heart-stopping moment

I thought they were going to tear into one another right then and there. I moved to stand between them. I placed a hand on Adam's chest, surprised to feel the panicked thudding of his heart beating against my palm. "It's okay. I'm fine. *We're* fine."

"Like hell!" Nick bit out. "She just told me I'm some kind of ... *beast!*"

Recognition flickered in Adam's eyes. He rolled his shoulders back and drew in a slow breath. "I'm sorry, Nick."

Nick looked up, surprised. "Save your pity, *dog*."

My mouth dropped open. Adam reached for my arm and dragged me back a step. "Holls, let's leave him alone for a minute. Give him some breathing room."

I started to argue but then followed Adam's unblinking gaze back to Nick. His posture hadn't relaxed. He looked ready to battle with anyone who got close enough. Was this the curse? Was he going to change right there in the sitting room?

For one insane moment, my eyes snapped to the heirloom pieces Posy had arranged through the space. She was going to lose her mind if one thing got damaged, and if Nick went full were, there wouldn't be a stick of furniture left in one piece when he was done.

"Adam, we can't—"

He pulled me with more force. "Now, Holly."

I twisted out of his grip and went to Nick. Adam lunged for me but I stepped out of the way at the last moment and he stumbled forward. With a snarl, he snapped out and grabbed my arm. "Holly, it isn't safe!"

Nick's eyes had gone ice blue. They shot from Adam to mine and then something changed. They flickered and changed back into the darker blue I was used to. "Holly?" he said, his voice shaky. He stumbled back toward the couch and collapsed on it. "What—what's happening to me?" He looked at Adam, who released my arm. "Adam, I don't know why I said that to you. I'm—gosh—I'm so sorry!"

My heart twisted in my chest when a sob tore from Nick. He buried his face in his hands, taking an extra beat to look at them, as though worried they'd turn to paws right before his eyes.

I craned around and looked up at Adam. His face was an unreadable mix of emotions. Shock, fear, anger, sadness, pity. They all flickered across his face as he watched Nick come undone.

I sat beside Nick on the couch and wrapped an arm tenderly around his bare shoulders. He turned into me and cried into my neck. "Holly, I'm sorry. I'm so sorry. I would never hurt you."

I nodded and made a soothing sound of agreement. "I know, Nick. I know."

But when I lifted my eyes to Adam I saw the same thought reflected back at me: Yes you would.

CHAPTER 25

It took some time, but eventually Nick succumbed to sleep. In all of the action, he'd managed to reopen his wounds and the bandage on his chest was soaked with fresh blood. Evangeline came in once things died down and applied more of the healing salve and redressed the deep gashes. He'd thanked her and then accepted a second dose of my sleeping potion. Minutes later, his eyes slid closed and his breathing leveled out.

Adam refused to leave my side the rest of the night, and the last thing I remembered was watching him as he sat on the floor beside my chair, his eyes trained on Nick. Even when I reached out and brushed his shoulder, he refused to look away. Aggressive energy poured from him. I didn't want to fall asleep and risk waking up to the two of them going at each other's throats. I hated the thought. The idea that someday there might come a point where I had to make the choice between saving myself or someone else, and sacrificing the life of one of my dearest friends—it was too ugly to even dwell on for more than a few seconds. In the end, my eyes were too heavy and I couldn't force them to stay open another minute.

The next day, I woke up in the chair beside the couch and found Nick still sleeping soundly. Adam looked over at me. "You're still awake?" I whispered.

"I had to make sure," was all he said.

"It has to be safe now," I replied softly. "The sun's up. Come on."

Adam looked at Nick once more and then pushed off the floor. He moved gingerly and I imagined his muscles were strained and sore from the fight with Ben the night before. In a way, it all seemed far away, like a horrible dream, but when I started to move, my own body reminded me that it wasn't. My legs cried out as I untucked them and stood. I stretched, cringing with each kink in my back and neck.

"Gorgeous, I'm getting too old for this badass routine," Adam said once we were in the hallway.

I closed the door to the sitting room and smiled up at him. "You always say that."

He chuckled and looped an arm around my waist. "You think Nick's going to be okay?"

I sighed heavily. "We're going to have to help him."

Adam gave a solemn nod.

Evangeline, Teddy, Lacey, and Posy were all gathered around the table when we pushed into the kitchen. They all looked up when we entered, a single question etched on their faces.

"He's still asleep," I said.

Adam gestured for me to take a seat while he went across the kitchen to pour two mugs of coffee. He set a mug in front of me and then took the chair beside me.

No one knew what to say, not even enough to attempt small talk. The heaviness of the night before hung thick in the air and sucked all the normal levity from our morning routine. Lacey was the first to leave. It was past her normal bedtime. She wished us all well on her way out.

You know things are bad when Lacey is overly polite.

Moments later, a knock on the front door interrupted the mostly silent meal. Adam got up to answer it and came back to the kitchen a minute later. He held the door open. "Holly, someone to see you."

Agent Bramble appeared in the doorway.

Adam waved her through and then left, Evangeline and Posy following him.

"Would you like some coffee?" I asked her once the door swung shut.

"Sure. Black, please. I don't do anything fancy in my coffee."

Why didn't that surprise me?

I poured her a mug and sat back down once she was seated. "I want to thank you again for coming to my rescue last night, Agent Bramble."

"Just doing my job, Holly."

"Well thank you, anyway."

"In some ways, I should be thanking you." She turned the coffee mug in her hands. "Without your help, Dune Kasey would have likely taken the fall for a terrible crime he didn't commit. Not to mention Sasha Pringle would still be sitting on the council. There's no telling how much damage she may have done in the course of her career."

"What will happen to her?"

"She's in SPA custody and will remain there until a formal trial. You will likely be called to testify as to the events of last night. Her lackey, Benjamin, has already agreed to testify in exchange for protection. It appears he was acting under her control when his crimes were committed and is not being held responsible."

I nodded. I still had mixed feelings about Ben, especially

considering the permanent scars his actions would have on Nick's life. But I wasn't going to push the issue. As long as I never had to see him again, I didn't really care what they did with him.

"What about Agent Mache and Bill Praxle?"

Agent Bramble frowned as she took a sip of coffee. "That's stickier. I've documented your testimony on that matter but there will have to be a formal investigation. As to Mr. Praxle's current council hearing, the council members will be advised of the new investigation and made aware that any attempts at SPA interference are unacceptable."

I frowned. I wasn't sure that would do much good. It was impossible to say how many council members resided in the pocket of either Mache or Praxle, but that was someone else's battle. I was taking myself out of the game. My only intention had been to get justice for Harvey. I'd done that and was ready to move on, even if I still hadn't managed to figure out what my future would look like. The immediate future was clear; taking care of Nick and making sure he survived the transition to his new life as a werewolf.

As if sensing my thoughts, Agent Bramble raised the topic. "The man who was wounded by the werewolf. He's a friend of yours?"

I nodded, unsure whether I should volunteer that he was only a few rooms away.

"He will need to fill out some paperwork with the SPA. Can I count on you to walk him through that process?"

"Yes. I've already explained the basics to him. I'll bring him to headquarters when it's time."

"Thank you."

We sipped our coffee and when Agent Bramble finished hers, she took the mug to the sink and rinsed it out. I smiled after her, wondering if she was even fully aware of what she was doing, or if the habit was so ingrained she did it without thinking.

"Before I go, there's one more thing." She turned back toward me, crossed the kitchen, and reached into the bag she'd hung on the back of her chair. She flipped through what sounded like a stack of paperwork and then pulled out a single sheet. She kept it face down, against her body for a moment. "Your petition to receive your potions master license has been approved."

"My what?"

"Harriet found paperwork in Harvey's case notes that states his desire for you to receive your license and be allowed to live within haven society. These notes are quite old. It appears that was always his intention for you. In honor of his memory, the SPA has worked with the Haven Council to grant this as something of a final request."

She turned the paper over and there, embossed in dark whorls of ink, was the thing I'd been waiting for all my life. Tears sprang to the corners of my eyes as they poured over the lines and lettering.

My fingers shook as I reached for the glossy certificate. "Is this real?"

She inclined her head and offered a soft smile. "You're officially free to live whatever life you choose, Holly. My advice? Choose wisely."

~

Nearly three weeks passed before Nick was willing to talk about what had happened in that alley. He stayed with us at the manor for a few days, spending most of that time asleep. One morning, he came to breakfast with the rest of us as we prepared to start our days and announced he was going home. He thanked us for all of our help and then he was gone.

Adam advised me to give him space, but I couldn't bear the thought of leaving him alone. So instead, I visited him every few days. Usually for only for a few minutes—always armed with his favorite espresso drink and a handful of day-old leftovers from the coffee shop. I didn't needle him into talking about the attack. I didn't know how to start. There wasn't exactly an etiquette guide for talking to newly cursed weres. Perhaps someone should write one. *Approaching Baby Werewolves and Other Tricky Paranormal Problems.*

He'd been friendly, although a little less so than before the attack. He was present physically, smiled and nodded on cue, but it was clear his mind was somewhere else entirely.

One night, I went to see him after my shift with a bag of muffins in one hand and a mocha in the other. When I arrived at his office, I found the door locked. No lights on behind the frosted glass. With a sad sigh I turned and left. When I arrived back at the manor I was surprised to find him waiting on the front steps. His face was downcast, filled with shadows cast from the soft lights surrounding the wrap around porch.

"Nick?" I said softly. I took careful steps up the walk, as though I would spook him if I moved faster. "What are you doing here?"

He looked up and tried a smile. It didn't quite reach his eyes. "Work was slow today so I closed up early. Wandered around town for a little while and somehow wound up here. I'm not even really sure why. Apparently this place is some kind of homing beacon for me."

I smiled gently and took my place beside him on the porch. "Well I was going to pawn these goodies off on Adam, but what he doesn't know won't hurt him." I handed him the mocha and placed the bag of muffins between us on the steps.

"Thanks, Holly. You really don't have to keep this up."

I frowned. "I'm not *keeping anything up*. You're my friend and I like doing things that make you happy."

He gave a small nod and sipped at the drink. "Well thank you. I probably don't say it enough, but I appreciate it. I appreciate you."

We fell into a comfortable silence. After a few moments, I dug into the bag and selected the top muffin. It didn't matter which flavor it was; I liked them all. I peeled back the wrapper and a burst of blueberry and lemon tickled my nose. "Is there no one home?" I asked, peering over my shoulder to look up at the manor. The lights were on, but they usually were. Posy said just because she was a ghost didn't mean she wanted to be left in the dark when we were all out for the evening. Ironic, because she often barricaded herself in the attic where there wasn't much more than a single bare light bulb that was never turned on as far as I knew.

"I'm not sure," Nick answered. "I didn't knock. I got here and just needed a minute to think, I guess."

I nodded as if I understood, although I wasn't sure I did, at least not fully.

"How are you doing with everything?"

He released a breath of a laugh. "The million-dollar question, huh?"

I didn't reply.

"I wish I had an answer for you, Holly. I really do."

"It's a lot to take in. I wish I could tell you it's all going to work itself out, but I can't. What I can say is that we're all here for you, no matter what happens next."

He nodded but kept his gaze trained ahead, staring into the neighborhood as night approached. I fell silent again and nibbled on pieces of muffin, breaking them apart with my fingers. I was scattering more crumbs than I was actually eating, mostly just to have something to do with my hands.

"All this time, Holly." Nick shook his head, dazed. "It was all real. Right there under my nose."

I remained silent. In light of everything that had happened over the past few weeks, I knew there was nothing I could add that would take away the shock he was feeling.

Nick turned to me. "You remember that first night we met?"

I laughed. "How could I forget?"

A smile pulled at one corner of his lips. "You threatened to pull a gun on me but it turned out your biggest weapon was a chubby cat. You weren't even wearing shoes capable of doing any damage. I'm pretty sure you were wearing fuzzy bunny slippers..."

I elbowed him. "I was *not* wearing fuzzy bunny slippers."

He chuckled and stared out at the street in front of the manor. "I came here, sneaking around, hoping to find some haunted house. That was what brought me to Beechwood in the first place. I thought there were ghosts living here and that I'd crack open some dark secret and write a tell-all book that would be turned into a movie franchise!"

"You never told me that part."

He shrugged. "It was a pipe dream. The silly place my mind wandered when I was frustrated with life."

I gave him an understanding nod. I had a few of those myself.

"I never thought any of this would happen, Holly."

"I know."

"I don't know how I'm supposed to feel about any of this, you know? On the one hand, all of my suspicions turned out to be true. I wasn't completely crazy thinking there was some other world just under the surface. But now, whether I want to be or not, I'm a part of that world and I can't go back to my old one ever again."

"I wish I could have prepared you for this. You don't know how many times I've wondered if maybe I should have told you the truth a long time ago, back when we first became friends. There were dozens of moments it nearly tumbled out of my mouth."

He turned at that. I felt his eyes staring at my profile. "Why didn't you?"

I sighed. "I guess that's *my* million-dollar question. In part, it's against haven law. Now, I'm not *entirely* opposed to breaking—or at least fudging the lines—of the law. But some part of me worried that you wouldn't believe me. As curious as you were about ghosts and all that, I also got this feeling that to you, it was still something fantastical. I didn't know how you would react and I didn't want to risk our friendship in case you didn't believe me."

He gave a thoughtful nod. "I'm not sure what I would have said to you. There's a good chance I would have called you crazy and avoided eye contact at the grocery store."

"Sounds about right." I laughed. "Hey, why don't you come in and have dinner?"

Nick shook his head. "Thanks but I don't think I'm quite ready for all that just yet. If you don't mind, I'd rather stay here."

"Sure. You're always welcome here, Nick. Especially now that I'm not worried about you walking in mid-Lacey and Adam showdown."

He smiled at me. "As a werewolf, whose side should I pick there?"

I blinked, surprised at the casual way he referenced his new identity. He hadn't said it that plainly since finding out the news. I took it as a good sign and smiled. "I have to pick

Adam's because, ya know, kind of the girlfriend code. So you can take Lacey's and we'll start betting on their matches."

Nick laughed. "Sounds like a plan."

I pushed up from the porch, brushed a hand over Nick's shoulders, and said goodnight. Inside, Adam was standing at the large picture window in the living room, one hand buried in a bag of trail mix.

"You think he's going to be okay?" he asked when I joined him. I followed his gaze and saw that Nick was still sitting on the porch, staring out into the night. A shiver of doubt snaked through me.

I tore my eyes off Nick's slumped silhouette and glanced at Adam. "I really don't know."

Adam looped an arm around me and pulled me gently into his side. "We'll help him through it."

I nodded sadly. "We'll do our best."

The moon hovered in the inky sky, bright and yet somehow ominous with Nick sitting beneath it. Within a couple of days, it would be full and Nick would face his first change since being cursed. Adam had already agreed to run the forest with him during the full moon. He tried to play it off, saying it was to keep Nick out of trouble, but we all knew the truth. He would be there to make sure Nick didn't hurt anyone.

"Who knows, now that you've got your potions license, maybe you'll be the one to find the cure for the curse."

I smiled up at Adam. "Pretty sure that's giving me way too much credit, but thank you."

He dropped a kiss to my forehead.

"Thank you," I said.

"For what?"

"For always being here. No matter what new insanity is unleashed around us."

Adam grinned. "Is this your way of warning me to buckle up again?"

I laughed. "You never know what's waiting around the corner. After all, now that Nick knows the truth about all of us, maybe he'll want to get back to his paranormal investigator roots."

"And if he does, how would that involve you?" Adam asked, though I suspected we both already knew the answer.

I shrugged one shoulder. "He might need a partner. Someone to show him the ropes of the supernatural world."

Adam cringed. "I was afraid you'd say that."

I popped up onto my tiptoes and kissed him. "Come on! How much trouble could we really get into?"

Groaning, he kissed me back, then leaned his forehead against mine. "Please don't make me think about the answer to that question."

Author's Note:

Thank you so much for diving back into Beechwood Harbor! I hope you enjoyed your stay.

Holly's adventures continue in Along Came a Ghost, a novella that introduces a sassy new heroine and solves an old mystery. Be sure to check it out!

As always, reviews make a huge difference and I would appreciate if you would take a few minutes to leave a quick note.

Until next time,
Danielle Garrett
www.DanielleGarrettBooks.com

ACKNOWLEDGMENTS

First of all, I would like to thank my parents, who fed my love of reading from an early age. My sister, for supporting my desire to tell stories since I started "over complicating" our Barbie doll's lives.

For my handsome husband, you know how much I love you. I appreciate your daily support (and for listening to all of my writerly rants and keeping my caffeinated at all times).

Thank you to Theresa, my fabulous editor for all of your tips and kind words. And Keri, for the killer covers.

Writing can be a solitary passion, but with all of you beside me, it's never lonely.

Thank you.

ABOUT DANIELLE GARRETT

From a young age, Danielle Garrett was obsessed with fantastic places and the stories set within them. As a lifelong bookworm, she's gone on hundreds of adventures through the eyes of wizards, princesses, elves, and some rather wonderful everyday people as well.

Danielle now lives in Oregon and while she travels as often as possible, she wouldn't want to call anywhere else home. She shares her life with her husband and their house full of animals, and when not writing, spends her time being a house servant for three extremely spoiled cats and one outnumbered puppy.

For more about Danielle and her work, please visit her at:
www.daniellegarrettbooks.com
www.facebook.com/daniellegarrettbooks

CPSIA information can be obtained
at www.ICGtesting.com
Printed in the USA
LVOW07s2130041217
558590LV00004B/1088/P